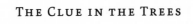

THE CLUE IN THE TREES

ALSO BY MARGI PREUS
PUBLISHED BY THE UNIVERSITY OF MINNESOTA PRESS

Enchantment Lake: A Northwoods Mystery

THE CLUE IN THE TREES

AN ENCHANTMENT LAKE MYSTERY

MARGI PREUS

UNIVERSITY OF MINNESOTA PRESS

Minneapolis · London

Lines from the poem "The Scent of Fresh Wood" by Hans Børli, translated by Robert Ferguson, are used with the permission of Aschehoug, Norway.

Published by the University of Minnesota Press
111 Third Avenue South, Suite 290
Minneapolis, MN 55401-2520
http://www.upress.umn.edu

ISBN 978-1-5179-0219-3 (hc)
ISBN 978-1-5179-0220-9 (pb)
A Cataloging-in-Publication record for this book is available from the Library of Congress.

Printed in the United States of America on acid-free paper

The University of Minnesota is an equal-opportunity educator and employer.

22 21 20 19 18 17   10 9 8 7 6 5 4 3 2 1

CONTENTS

I

SOMETHING IS NOT RIGHT

A METALLIC CRASH jarred Francie out of slumber. She sat up in bed and listened. The fridge hummed; the clock ticked; the bathroom fan whirred. Rain tapped lightly against the window. Her heart thumped a little harder than usual. Something was not right. The apartment felt . . . wrong.

Where had that crash come from? She scanned what was visible of the small apartment. From her bed she could see the tiny kitchen, where a red pinprick on the coffeemaker cast a small but eerie circle of light. An overly bright nightlight flickered in the hall. The light on her computer pulsed green. The numbers 3:03 glowed on the clock in her dark bedroom.

Another crash. Definitely outside her bedroom window. She lifted the window shade and peered down at the alley at a couple of overturned garbage cans. A black shape pawed at one of them. A dog? A *big* dog? No—it was a bear!

The beast's head disappeared into the can and reemerged

with something in its jaws, then slunk away, its wet fur glistening as it passed under the streetlight.

Francie flopped back on the bed and laughed. In Brooklyn she'd been accustomed to noise: sirens, horns blasting, traffic, and the sound of bottles being tossed into dumpsters at 2:00 a.m., but definitely not marauding bears. Only in a little northwoods town like Walpurgis.

"Just a bear," she told herself. "Go back to sleep." She needed to sleep! Tomorrow—well, technically today—would be the first day of her senior year in high school, in a brand-new school in a brand-new town. It would be preferable to start it with a decent night's sleep.

The numbers on the bedside clock glowed, unblinking as a tiger's green-eyed stare—3:06. She glared at it, but the clock refused to be intimidated, taunting her by winking and flipping to 3:07. This splot of light, the nightlight, the glowing computer, the dot of light on the coffeemaker, wouldn't have attracted her attention at all if she hadn't spent the summer at her great-aunts' lake cabin where there was no electricity and a whole lot of quiet—and at night, a whole lot of dark.

She turned away from the clock and pressed her eyes shut. Immediately, they sprang open again. There was still something not right. She was, she felt suddenly certain, not alone.

Francie slowly drew back the covers, quietly rose, slipped a bathrobe over her pajamas, tiptoed through the still unfamiliar apartment, past the bathroom with its whirring fan, into the kitchen where she picked up a frying pan, then past the nightlight, noticing the long shadow she cast on the opposite wall as she went by, and into the living room, where she could clearly see a dark shape hunkered on the couch.

Her first thought was: the bear got in and is sitting on my couch. Her next thought was: that is not a bear.

2

MUSKIE BAIT

A FLASH OF LIGHTNING illuminated the room, and Francie saw who was really sitting there. "Ever heard of a doorbell?" she asked.

"Sis!" The lump on the couch leaped up and hugged Francie. "Didn't want to wake you," he said. "Figured I'd just crash on your couch and say hi in the morning."

"Theo, you big lug," Francie said and punched him. "I thought you were a bear! No wonder—look how long your hair is! Where have you been, anyway?"

Thunder rattled the windowpane. Theo crossed the room to the window and pried open the venetian blinds. "You know that old bait store?" he asked, peeking out. "The one inside the giant muskie?"

"Muskie Bait? *That's* where you've been for the past three years?"

"No, but do you remember where it is?"

"Sure, it's—"

"Come on." Theo turned and took her hand. "Show me."

"Now?"

"Now, and out the back entrance of this place."

Francie threw a jacket over her robe and slid on a pair of sneakers while Theo pulled his long, curly hair into a ponytail. Then they ran down the back stairway and out into the rain. Thunder rolled in the distance.

"No car," he said. "We'll go on foot."

As she led him down the wet streets of the small town, she glanced over her shoulder. A dark figure trailed them. "Is that guy following us?" she asked.

Theo didn't bother to look. "Yeah." He took her arm and veered sharply off the street. "I'll explain later."

They turned down an alley, sidled between a couple of houses, dashed through some backyards, ducked under a swing set, climbed over a fence, and ran across a parking lot until they stood in front of a giant plaster fish.

Lightning crackled and pulsed, illuminating the fish's gaping jaws with its damp, shadowy interior and huge plaster teeth.

"Well, there it is," Francie said. "But I'm not going in there, if that's what you're thinking." She cast a distrustful eye at those jagged teeth.

Another, much closer, heart-stopping bolt of lightning sent her and Theo scuttling into the muskie's open mouth.

It was weird standing around inside a fish, Francie thought, even though she knew it was just the entry to a kitschy gift shop. It was especially eerie in the middle of a stormy night with rain lashing against the fish's scaly sides.

She was so tired she wondered if she was actually asleep and dreaming, dreaming she had been swallowed by a giant muskellunge and pulled underwater. She could almost feel the tugging of the current and the rolling action of the waves. Also, she was rain-soaked enough to have drowned.

"Do you think it's possible to survive in the belly of a whale?" Francie asked, as Theo groped around the inside of the mouth.

When Theo didn't answer, Francie went on. "Seriously, though, what is going on? Like, why are we being chased by a guy in a trench coat and a fedora? I mean, who dresses like that in a backwater Minnesota town like this?"

The only reply was the sound of Theo's shoes scraping on the concrete floor as he ran his hands along the muskie's teeth.

"No need to answer, Theo," Francie said. "The answer can be summed up in one word: you. After being gone from my life for the past three years, you show up—not at any ordinary time of day, but in the middle of the night, the night before the first day of my senior year—my senior year in a brand-new high school!"

"Which belly did you mean?" Theo asked, then disappeared down the length of the fish.

"What?" Francie heard the sound of a door being rattled. "I'm sure the gift shop is locked," she called to him, stumbling toward the sound.

"Here, hold this," Theo said. She felt his backpack being thrust into her hands. "A whale has four stomachs," he said, jiggling the door handle.

Francie tried to peer over his shoulder at whatever he was doing. Jimmying the door? Picking the lock is what it looked like. "You know that's locked, right?" she said.

"The first stomach has no digestive juices," Theo went on, continuing with whatever he was doing to the door handle. "The stomach muscles flex and crush the food. So assuming you got swallowed only as far as the first stomach, you might actually be able to survive, as long as you could escape the muscle mastication. If you made it as far as stomach number two, you'd have to share it with undigested squid beaks. A lot of them. As many as eighteen thousand. All of which have to be vomited out."

"Is it even possible to be swallowed by a whale?" Francie watched Theo's hands intently, because knowing how to open a locked door could come in extremely handy. Particularly, Francie thought, since there was a specific locked door that she really *really* wanted to open.

"If a sperm whale can swallow a giant squid, which it can, it can swallow a person, if it wanted to," Theo said. "But why would it want to?"

The lock made a satisfying clicking sound and Theo pushed the door open. Francie wondered where and when he had learned that trick. Bells on the door jingled as Theo pulled Francie inside the store and closed the door behind them.

"Okay, you still haven't told me what is going on!" Francie said. "This is what you always do," she whispered accusingly. "You just start talking about something else. Even when we were kids, if you didn't want to talk about the subject, you'd get off on some obscure topic."

"You brought up the topic of whales," Theo reminded her. He took his backpack from her and slipped it on.

"Yes, but only you would make a whole conversational issue out of it, especially when there are more important things to discuss."

"Like squids, for instance," Theo said, dragging Francie farther into the store.

"See? That's exactly what I'm talking about. You've done that our whole lives! Like whenever I asked about Mom, you'd change the subject, detour, refuse to let go of an unrelated tack you were on, whatever!"

"Now let's see if there's a back door to this place," he said.

"See?" Francie said. "See? You're doing it again."

The bells on the door jingled, and Theo gave Francie's arm an urgent squeeze.

"Didn't you lock the door behind us?" Francie whispered. A rack of key rings rattled as she backed into it.

In answer, Theo yanked her past the mugs and plates down the aisle toward the stuffed animals.

Francie heard the clicking of footsteps hurrying after them. As they ran, Theo grabbed things off the shelves and threw them behind him, littering the aisle with ashtrays and stuffed animals.

Still their pursuer was gaining on them. Although in the dim light Francie could barely see the person, she could hear the nylon rustle of a trench coat. She snatched fluffy bears and soft antlered moose off the shelves and chucked them behind her.

"You might want to throw something with sharper edges!" Theo yelped, as he lobbed what looked like bags of pancake mix at their pursuer—confirmed when on impact they exploded in puffs of powdery smoke.

Now the man—it was a man, she could tell that—was right behind her, breathing heavily. Groping the shelves for something, anything, Francie's hand grazed bottles maybe, or jars, then gallon-sized tins of she wasn't sure what, but she grabbed one and, when the man ducked to avoid an oncoming bag of pancake mix, she swung at his fedora.

There was the crunch of aluminum, a groan, the spattering of sticky liquid, the heavy smell of maple, the thud of a body slumping to the floor, then a steady glugging sound.

Theo pulled Francie out the front door, through the fish's throat, and, ducking a little to avoid the muskie's teeth, the two of them shot out of its mouth, onto the street, and disappeared into the night.

3

AT SCHOOL

FRANCIE BLINKED, trying to keep her eyes from closing in third-hour English class. She'd held it together during first hour, powered through second-hour chemistry, and was just drifting off when she heard the teacher, Ms. Broderick, telling the class how "Francesca solved several . . ." A flood of what felt like ice water raced through Francie's veins, and she sat up and gripped the seat with her fingers. ". . . murders out at Enchantment Lake!" Ms. Broderick finished. "Our own Northwoods Nancy Drew!" she chirped and pointed at Francie. "Can you tell us about that, Francesca?"

All the students turned to stare at her. Francie, caught off guard, stared back, thinking, *Nancy Drew? Are you kidding me?*

"Um . . . ," she said, stupidly.

Ms. Broderick urged her along, saying, "Of course, I'm talking about the mystery that you solved last summer."

"I didn't really solve anything, actually," Francie said.

"But you brought the murderer to justice!" the teacher exclaimed.

"Totally by accident," Francie said.

"And of course there's the exciting discovery you made of the mastodon bones!"

"No!" Francie squawked. "I really didn't discover—"

"I hope we'll hear all about it," the teacher went on, "the end of this week when your papers are due."

Paper? She must have slept through that assignment. Was she really supposed to write about how she spent her summer vacation? Somehow she did not think anyone would be interested in hearing how she'd sort of pretended to be a detective—made easier by her aunts telling everyone that she was one—and going snooping in all the wrong places, and being in the wrong place at the wrong time and almost getting herself and a couple of other people killed. Well, maybe that last part would be interesting. And there had been a fire, an explosion, a poisoned hotdish, a lost kayak, a blindfolding, a couple of scary boat rides, and, of course, murder. And then those bones. That was pretty cool, too. Okay, maybe it was sort of exciting.

The bell rang, the students rose like a flock of sparrows, closing books and notebooks in a flutter, gathering up loose items and sliding into jackets.

"You don't seem like the angry vandal type," the girl sitting behind Francie said, as she rose from her desk.

"What?" Francie spun around to look at her.

"That Muskie Bait thing?" the girl said. "That wasn't you?"

Francie did not want to lie. It was not in her nature to lie and she rarely did, even though right now lying seemed like the least of her crimes. So she evaded the question. "What makes you think that?" she said.

"You've got maple syrup in your hair."

Francie grabbed at a hank of her hair and examined the ends—clumped with dried syrup. "That's probably from breakfast," she explained.

The girl tilted her head and squinted, as if trying to imagine how one got syrup on the back of one's head while eating breakfast, then said, "I'm too polite to ask." She smiled, a not unkind smile. Francie was grateful for that.

Then, as if in answer to Francie's unasked question—which would have been "How do you know about Muskie Bait?"—the girl said, "My dad's a cop."

Great, Francie thought. Today is starting off just great.

Francie went straight to the bathroom where she stuck her head in the sink and scrubbed the syrup out of her hair. She was dimly aware of girls going in and out, but none of them said anything. When she got the sticky stuff out, she dried her hair as best she could under the hand drier.

On the way to lunch, she walked slowly through the halls, which seemed to be buzzing with news of some kind.

"The town is crawling with them!" someone said.

Francie wanted to ask, "With whom?" but didn't want to be the weird kid who barges into other people's conversations while using archaic, if proper, grammar. So she kept her ears open as she continued down the hall past the band room where what sounded like a pep band was practicing. She stood for a moment listening: a few bars, a blatantly bad chord, music stopped, peals of laughter, back to music. It made her wish she played an instrument. Then she could play in a band and at least belong to a group.

As she listened, a cluster of students walked by.

"... the FBI!" Francie heard, and "... smuggling ..."

She also heard "maple syrup," which she assumed was about her, and "Customs and Immigration—the Canadian ones."

Figures, Francie thought. It's probably Theo causing all this trouble, being trailed by law enforcement from the entire Western Hemisphere. No, she thought, that is too ridiculous. There must be something else going on.

Her attention was diverted to the posters that plastered the walls advertising openings on the debate team, a speech tournament, and auditions for the play *Antigone*.

She paused. They were going to tackle Greek tragedy? Would it be awful? Or maybe the question should be, "How awful?"

"Interested?" said a voice behind her. Francie turned to see a boy smiling at her. "Auditions are on Tuesday."

"I'm impressed," Francie said. "I mean, you guys are going to do *Antigone*?"

"Oh, is that how you say it? An-TIG-uh-nee? We've been saying ANTY-gone."

She laughed. "I probably would, too, but we studied it in school."

"Where did you go to school?"

"Brooklyn," she said.

"Brooklyn? As in New York?"

"Yeah, that Brooklyn, but I grew up spending summers here, or at a lake near here."

"Enchantment?"

"Yeah," Francie said. "How did you know that?"

"I'm guessing you're the famous detective," he said.

Before Francie could protest, a head-splitting electronic blare rang out: the bell.

The boy started walking backwards down the hall. "We're going out to Enchantment today!" he called back to her. "The director is taking some of us theater kids out to see that archaeological site—I guess he's friends with the guy in charge out there. Sort of a field trip. Maybe I'll see you there?" Then he bashed into a wall of lockers. He turned to shake his fist at the lockers, smiled back at Francie, then disappeared down the hall.

So now, Francie thought, time to face lunch, probably the most awkward time of day in a new school where you don't know anyone. But there was no skipping it—she hadn't had breakfast and she was starving. If she didn't eat lunch, there was no way she'd make it through the rest of the day.

In the lunch line, she pushed her tray along, trying not to make eye contact with any of the girls ahead of her, in case they'd been in the bathroom just now. It was hard to tell what lunch was, exactly.

"Beans?" a gravelly voice behind the steam trays asked.

Francie glanced up and nodded, then paused. She looked at the lady scooping green beans—had she seen her somewhere before? Weird. The lunch lady plunked a scoop of grayish green beans onto Francie's plate while eyeing her with distaste.

What's she got against me? Francie wondered, continuing down the line, being served some brownish lumps that possibly had once been part of a cow, a bun, a limp pickle, and a dish of gray pudding with a dollop of none-too-white whipped cream on top. Putty-flavored pudding with a garnish of grout, anyone?

A table full of girls went suddenly silent when Francie walked by, and as soon as she'd moved just a few steps past their table, she heard one of them whisper, "She washed her hair in the bathroom sink!"

Then another said, "And dried it under the hand drier!"

Just great, she thought for the hundredth time that day. Her senior year was starting out just great.

Francie sat down at a mostly empty table—a few strays at the other end who looked like freshmen were hopefully too intimidated to say anything to her—and she started in on . . . beans and whatever else her lunch was.

She had just stuck a forkful of it into her mouth when the girl who'd brought up the maple syrup situation slid into the seat across from her.

"Hey, I'm sorry if I freaked you out about the Muskie Bait thing," the girl said. "I'm not going to turn you in or anything."

"That's nice of you," Francie said, hoping her tablemate caught the irony in her voice.

"Jay says you might try out for the play."

"What play?" Francie said. "Who's Jay?"

"The guy you met in the hall, by the audition poster. You should totally try out."

"No, I don't think so," Francie said. "But thanks."

"It's a good way to meet people. I just started at this school last year—used to go to school on the rez—and I didn't like it here until I got into doing plays and stuff. It can be hard to make friends. My name's Raven, by the way," the girl said, holding out her hand.

Francie shook it. Except for her dark hair, Raven didn't seem very raven-like. She didn't seem fierce, large, or raucous, which is what Francie thought of when she thought of the big black birds. Maybe she should have been named Sparrow. The girl was pretty enough, with her coffee-with-cream complexion, but wearing a nondescript shirt and jeans, neither in nor out of style, she seemed like the kind of person who strives to go unnoticed. Except for her earrings.

"I like your earrings," Francie said, hoping to keep the conversation off auditions and/or vandalism, and anyway, she did like them.

Raven put her fingers on the earrings as if to check what she was wearing. "Yeah," she said. "My grandma makes these out of porcupine quills. I help her pull quills sometimes."

"Wait. What? You pull quills out of porcupines?" Francie tried to picture it.

Raven laughed. "Well, they're not alive when we do it," she said.

"Good," Francie said, then turned her attention to trying to figure out what to do with the food—if it was food—on her tray.

"That's beef stew, I'm pretty sure," Raven said. "Want another recommendation? Bring a lunch from home." She smiled and held up her sandwich and said, "Cheers!"

Francie toasted her with a forkful of stew.

"Might go out to my grandma's this weekend, if you want the once-in-a-lifetime opportunity to pull quills," Raven said.

Francie busied herself trying to open a packet of salad dressing, then slowly squeezed out its contents. She appreciated the invitation, and she was kind of curious, but she wasn't sure how to respond. It wasn't that Raven was clearly not one of the "popular" girls—obvious, since she was sitting here with her, Francie the Weirdo, who washed her hair in the bathroom sink. No, what was really stopping her was that Raven's dad was a cop. And Francie was now a criminal.

A couple of boys went by, carrying their lunch trays. "Hey, Craven," said one, over his shoulder, "who let you out of jail?"

Raven rolled her eyes but otherwise ignored them as they went by, chuckling at their own attempt at wit.

Jail? Francie wondered. The first person she meets on her first day of school just got out of jail? Francie knew she should hardly judge—*she* probably ought to be in jail after last night. If her granddad found out about any of this, he'd yank her out of this school and this town and away from Enchantment so fast she wouldn't have time to blink.

4

AT ENCHANTMENT

THERE WAS SOMETHING beautifully melancholy about fall, Francie thought, as she and Theo motored out to the cabin later that afternoon. Leaves drifted from the trees and clustered along the shoreline or floated on the water, made suddenly so much colder by frosty nights. Some of the trees had already burst into the Walpurgis school colors: red and gold. These colors now shimmered up from the lake, reflected in the water. Farther up the hill, bare branches revealed lonely cabins, their windows shuttered. Docks had been taken in and stacked on the shore, summer residents gone south or wherever they went in the winter.

"Cool that there's still no road on this side of the lake," Theo said. "And that you still have to boat over to get there."

Francie nodded, then tried to cut to the chase. "Are you going to explain what happened last night?" She'd already grilled him on where he'd been the past three years ("All over the place") and what he'd been doing there ("This and that"), and now she was trying for a direct answer.

"Yeah, I'll explain that," Theo said, pointing at the motor and then his ears. Speaking over a running motor meant shouting, so, okay, Francie could see why he didn't want to talk about it now.

Francie glanced up at a wavering line of geese honking and barking their way across the sky.

"Pretty crazy having an archaeological dig going on here, huh?" Theo shouted. "Was it you who discovered the mastodon bones?"

"No, not me," Francie said. "And it seemed cool for a while, but it's getting old. A lot of people coming and going, for one thing, and the director of the dig is not exactly . . . popular, so everybody is grumpy. Theo, you're evading my questions." She pushed back the hair that blew around her face. "Just like you always did when I asked about Mom."

"Sometimes it's better not to know," Theo said.

"No, it isn't!" Francie wanted to shout, but she restrained herself. She felt that not knowing about her mother had been like a kind of blindness. Like some essential part of her had been stolen away.

"How was school?" Theo asked.

"What do *you* think?" Francie said.

"I'm sorry," Theo said. "Not enough sleep? My fault. But it'll get better, right? Can't get worse?"

She shrugged.

"Meet any nice kids?" Theo asked.

"I met a couple people. They were okay. There's an audition for a play," she said.

"You're going to try out, aren't you?"

"No."

"Why not? It would be a great way to get to know some people and do something you enjoy, too. I'm sure they'd be thrilled to get you. With your experience, you'd probably get the lead."

"That would be terrible!"

"Why terrible?"

Francie groaned. "I'm sure there's some girl who finally has a shot at the lead because the girl who always used to get the big parts has finally graduated, and then some stupid girl from New York comes and takes it away? That is *not* a good way to make friends."

"Ah," Theo said. "But it would still be fun to be in it."

"I don't think so," Francie said. "Rehearsals will be evenings and weekends. And those are the only times I have to come out here."

Theo slowed the motor on their approach to the dock, and Francie jumped at the opportunity to say, "I need to know about Mom, Theo."

"I know," Theo said, "and you're old enough." He cut the motor and eased the boat up to their aunts' dock, one of the few still in the water, then climbed out and tied up the boat. A sudden breeze caught Theo's long curls and billowed them around his face. He pulled the strands from his eyes and Francie unwound the scarf from her neck.

"When did your hair get so long?" she asked, playfully tying his hair back with her scarf. Touching his hair like that made her feel a rush of tenderness for him. When she was this close, she could see that what gave his hair its peculiar sheen was that among the thick black curls were bright, silvery hairs. "Your hair is turning white!" she cried.

"So's yours," he said, touching the streak of white that ran through her own dark hair.

"Which one of us will go all white first, do you think?" she mused, squinting out at the lake at a big raft of hooting and cooing loons. They came down from Canada or somewhere and gathered, hanging out in big groups before heading south, she remembered. She wished them well, the geese, the songbirds, the loons, on their long journey, hoping they could avoid windows, cars, cell towers, wind turbines, and giant glass football stadiums erected in their flight path. They had far to go and many obstacles in their way.

Out on the lake, beyond the loons, a pontoon full of teenagers plied the water toward the dock. Oh, brother. The field trip. Just when she was finally going to get Theo to tell her what she had waited her whole life to know. She shoved out of her mind the fact that she was the one who had gotten sidetracked on the subject of hair.

"But, Theo," she asked in a rush, "why were you old enough to know about Mom when you were little, but I wasn't? You've always known everything, haven't you?"

"Everything? No. But listen, Francie. You should be glad you didn't know. It was terrible having this secret all these years. Keeping a secret like that . . . it's not good. You're constantly evading questions—or just outright lying."

"I don't see why."

"Look. You're lucky to have been in the dark. For me, everything that came out of my mouth about her—about anything to do with her, our family, Dad—it began to seem like everything was a lie." He paused, then added, "It's not good to lie so much."

Francie was quiet for a moment. How could knowing be worse than not knowing? Well, she wasn't going to fight about it now. The sound of the pontoon was growing louder, along with the noise of the passengers.

"Having a few friends over?" Theo asked.

"I guess the theater kids are coming out here for some kind of field trip," Francie said.

"Theater field trip?"

"To see the dig."

"An archaeological play?"

"*Antigone.*"

"Oh . . . kay?" Theo said. "This isn't exactly ancient Greece out here."

"I don't get it either," Francie agreed.

As the two of them watched the boat's approach, Theo asked, "Why did you decide to stay here instead of going back to New York?"

"The aunts. The place. I don't know," Francie answered.

"A boyfriend?" Theo said.

"Oh, Nels?" Francie couldn't help sigh a little, thinking of him. "He's away at college anyway. So, no, that's not why I stayed. I was worried about Aunt Astrid and Aunt Jeannette after what happened this summer. I told Granddad I wanted to stay and finish school in Walpurgis and he agreed to pay the rent on a small apartment in town. 'As long as you keep those grades up,'" she added, speaking in her grandfather's gruff voice.

"I thought you were bound and determined to make it as an actor in New York."

"I was. But I'm only seventeen, and maybe I can just, you know, go to high school and be a regular, normal high school student in a normal, regular town."

"You, a normal, regular high school student?" Theo squinted at her.

There was another reason she had stayed, but she didn't know how to explain it, and anyway, there was an entire pontoon of theater kids arriving at their dock.

"Ahoy!" the one adult on board called out. The rest of the

crew, obviously making fun of him, began to talk as if it were Talk Like a Grizzled Seafarer Day.

The boat drew up to the dock, which put an end to brother and sister conversation. Francie recognized Sandy, from the resort across the lake, as the driver of the pontoon. She smiled and nodded and he gave a nod back, blushing as usual.

"Hi, Francie!" someone called. She looked into the group to see Jay—the guy she'd met by the audition poster—waving at her. She said hi and then noticed Raven, too, who also waved and said, "Hi, Francie!"

"You seem to have befriended half the school already," Theo said.

"Those are precisely the two people I met today," Francie explained as the students and the director filed off the boat onto the dock.

The girls, not surprisingly, ogled Theo as they went by, and Raven went so far as to whisper to Francie, "Is that your boyfriend?"

"Brother," Francie explained.

"Excellent!" Raven said, making Francie laugh. Raven laughed easily, too, and Francie felt herself warming to the girl. When Raven laughed, there was a glimpse of the raven hiding behind the sparrow's feathers. Her face glowed; her dark eyes gleamed with mischief.

The theater director introduced himself as Keith Redburn. "I hope it's okay that we landed at your dock? It's where Dr. Digby suggested we tie up. And sorry to ask, but could you show us to the site?"

"Maybe you can take them?" Theo suggested. "I have to greet the aunts before anything else happens. And drop off my bag." He held up his duffle.

"Plus, you don't know your way to the site," Francie added.

"Right," Theo said. He took the stairs up the hill two at a time and was gone.

Francie sighed and said, "Well, okay! Follow me, I guess."

Everyone except Sandy, who would stay with the boat, trooped after her up the hill and proceeded onto a well-traveled path that led through the woods back to the old bog where the archaeologists had been excavating. Raven walked with Francie and filled her in on why they were there: it turned out that one of the kids in the theater program—that one, Phoebe—had volunteered at the site this summer. Phoebe, Francie thought. Phoebe, Raven, Jay. Was *everyone* in this school named after a bird?

"But the main reason," Raven explained, "is that Mr. Redburn is friends with Dr. Digby, the director of the dig." Raven and Francie giggled over his name; then Raven went on. "They used to be college roommates or something, and I think Redburn wants to impress us with the people he knows, otherwise I have no idea what we're doing here."

"Mmm," Francie said, noncommittally. It was pretty likely they would all soon find out what kind of a jerk Digby was; he generally didn't waste any time making enemies. In fact, as they passed by Digby's tent—a large Boy Scout–style canvas tent on a wooden platform—Francie heard voices, Digby's and some other guy's, and sure enough, they were arguing. Digby hurled some kind of insult, and the other person said, ". . . if you spill the beans . . . ," before the group moved out of earshot.

The pit where the mastodon bones had been uncovered and mostly removed and hauled off somewhere now looked like, well, a pit.

"Is that it?" Raven asked.

"Yeah," Francie said. "They got a late start, but they'll work more on it next summer."

"Bo-ring," yawned one of the girls.

"Where are the bones? I thought we were going to see bones," Jay said.

"I guess they've been taken to . . ." Francie wasn't actually sure where they went. "The university? Or a museum?" She was feeling spectacularly ill-informed about everything and hoped one of the interns or college workers would rescue her. Unfortunately, a lot of the workers had left to go back to college. Just a few stragglers were left.

"Not like that, you imbecile!" a familiar voice shouted. It was Digby—tall and authoritative-looking, wearing a floppy canvas hat and sunglasses. He was directing orders at a girl in shorts, a safari-style shirt, and rubber boots, her blonde hair tucked into a bandana. He stopped her, sniffed, and gave her a good looking at. "Marly, isn't it?" he said.

"Mallory," she answered.

"Well, Melody, maybe you should just look for a wealthy husband—someone to support you. Archaeology is not a glamorous field," Digby said, rearranging the box she had been packing.

Mallory's jaws clenched and her nostrils flared. "Professor Digby," she said. "You have done nothing but insult me this whole entire summer, and I don't think I deserve it."

"The whole *entire* summer?" he repeated, clearly making fun of her. "So, shoot me," he finished, moving away.

"If looks could kill, Digby would be so dead right now," Raven whispered to Francie, flicking her eyes in the direction of Mallory, who was giving Digby a daggerlike glare.

Digby, however, had already moved on, shouting, "I'm surrounded by fashion models and incompetent fools! How am I supposed to accomplish anything here?" He flung open the flap of his big canvas tent and disappeared inside.

One of the college students appeared, slightly out of breath, smiled, introduced himself as Jackson, then gestured to everyone to follow him.

Now that Jackson had taken over, Francie thought, she could leave, right? She dawdled a bit so her departure wouldn't seem so abrupt, then let the group drift on ahead of her while she turned to head back to the cabin. As she passed by the tent, she heard Digby arguing again. Nothing surprising there—sooner or later he argued with everyone. She herself had argued with him that summer when he made it clear she was not welcome in the area.

She was headed down the path when the other voice in the tent reached her ears and made her steps slow. The voice was familiar. Theo? That was strange; he'd only just arrived. Why would he be arguing with Digby? And already? Straining to listen, she crept back toward the tent, but by the time she got close enough to hear the words, the argument was over. She did not want to get caught eavesdropping by either Theo or Digby, so she skedaddled down the path.

Back at the cabin, her aunts were in a tizzy over Theo's arrival. Jeannette was digging in the refrigerator to find something special to make for dinner, and Astrid was opening and closing cupboard doors, probably out of sheer excitement.

"Frenchy, it's you!" Astrid said, calling Francie by her lake nickname. Somebody had started calling her French Fry. (How could it be resisted with a name like Francie Frye?) The name had gotten shortened to Frenchy, and now was, as she thought of it, her lake name. "How was school?" Astrid asked.

"Fine," Francie said.

Jeannette pulled her head out of the fridge to say hello and inquire after her courses and teachers.

Francie gave condensed answers and then asked, "Where did Theo go?"

"He went to take a look at the site. Didn't you see him?"

"No," she said honestly. She hadn't actually *seen* him.

"He'll be back soon. Isn't it so exciting to have him here?"

"Never a dull moment," Francie said, also quite honestly.

"Listen, dear, would you mind helping with dinner? We've invited Digby—"

"What?" Francie said. "Digby? Why?"

"Well, the whole crew is about to leave, aren't they, and their cook was done for the season, and we haven't had him yet for dinner. We're just trying to be nice."

"Digby, though? He's so horrible."

"Yes, he is, isn't he?" Astrid said. "Why did we invite him, Jenny?"

"Did Theo know you invited Digby?" Francie asked.

"Oh, now let's see," Astrid said. "Jenny, did you tell Theo we'd invited Digby? Such a funny name for an archaeologist, isn't it?"

Jeannette handed Francie a bowl of cookie dough and said, "I don't remember that I did. Oh, I hope he isn't rude to Theo! But why would he be?"

As Francie plopped dough on a cookie sheet, she wondered that very thing, but she didn't bring up the conversation she'd overheard. Out the kitchen window she watched the theater kids file out of the woods and down to the pontoon, a few stragglers lagging behind, Raven and Jay among them.

"Ooh!" Astrid crowed. "Should we invite the kids in for cookies?"

"No!" Francie cried.

"Wouldn't you like to get to know some of your classmates?"

"Tomorrow will be soon enough."

. . . . .

After Francie slid a sheet of cookies into the oven, she walked to the picture window that faced the lake. The pontoon was still moored there, the students either on the boat or the dock, apparently waiting for someone. She could hear their voices trailing up from the water. Laughter, a bit of a song, a few lines from a play she recognized.

The couch beckoned and Francie lay down, intending to just rest, but she fell asleep hard. When she woke, she could tell it was dark outside, and the smell of burned cookies lingered in the air.

"The cookies!" she cried, sitting up and throwing off the blanket that one of her aunts must have draped over her.

"Don't worry," Astrid said. "I rescued them."

It didn't smell like an entirely successful rescue, Francie thought, trying to get her bearings. The table was set, the pots sat atop the stove, burners off, and the aunts sat nearby, each holding a little glass of sherry. From the light still lingering on the lake, Francie could tell that the pontoon was gone.

"Did dinner happen already?" Francie asked. "Where is Theo?"

"No, we haven't had dinner," Jeannette said, paging through a magazine. "We're still waiting for Digby and Theo."

Remembering the heated exchange she'd heard between the two men, Francie felt a white-hot bolt of something—fear?—rush through her, and she leapt off the couch. It was irrational, she knew—what did she think had happened? Maybe, she thought, it was just the disorienting feeling of waking in the dark, her lack of sleep, the whole strange Muskie Bait thing the night before. But she couldn't shake the feeling.

Theo, she thought, was in trouble. She knew it. She could feel it. Why hadn't it dawned on her until this moment? She had been so concerned about herself and her first day of school that she had neglected to see it. And now what she was feeling was horrible, soul-shaking fear.

"I'll go look for Theo," she said, lunging for the door.

"I'm sure he'll be here soon," Jeannette said. "He said something about . . ."

But Francie was out the door, flashlight in hand. She felt as if she had been struck by lightning and a fire had ignited inside her. She barely heard her aunts' little squeaks of protest as she charged down the path to the bog.

It was darker under the trees, and she was glad she'd brought a flashlight. The site was quiet, as would be expected. The few remaining workers must have returned to their cabins.

So there was nobody here. That was her first thought. But her flesh prickled from her scalp practically to her toes, as if someone were watching her.

Okay, she told herself. It's dark, I'm in the woods. There's nothing and nobody here. I'm just being a scaredy-cat. She forced herself toward Digby's tent, the last place she'd heard Theo. But it's quiet now, she told herself. There's obviously nobody there; it would just be a waste of time. Plus, surrounded as it was by overarching trees, it looked somehow ominous.

Oh, for cry-eye! she thought. Of course I have to look. She approached the tent, lifted the tent flap, and, aiming the flashlight, peeked inside. The small, weak beam played over a desk, spilled papers, a body—wait! What? She slowly moved the light along what was certainly a prone body, facedown, arms strangely sprawled.

She could not force herself to even think the word *Theo*, but she steeled herself and stepped inside the tent, letting the flap fall behind her.

Instantly, she felt trapped, almost like she couldn't breathe. Her heart hammered so hard she could barely speak. "Hello?" she croaked out, just in case the prone body was . . . doing yoga or something?

Half the person's face was visible, and, fighting the urge to run away, she shone the beam on it. It took but a glance to tell that the person she was looking at could only be one thing: dead.

5

AN UNPLEASANT SURPRISE

THERE ON THE FLOOR lay the ghostly, grayish remains of Dr. Donald Digby. Relief that it wasn't Theo mixed with horror that it was Digby, and that he was dead.

Francie hurried down the path as fast as she could in the dark with a dying flashlight, stumbling over roots and pushing away branches. Still, it wasn't until she was well down the trail that she realized it was the wrong path—a path that didn't lead to her aunts' but some other cabin.

Okay, she thought. Okay . . . I'll just get to wherever it goes and then take the path along the lake to get back to the aunts'. It'll be all right . . . Unless I meet up with the killer! Why was she so sure Digby had been killed and hadn't just had a heart attack? She hadn't seen any blood or really any evidence of foul play. Well, she hadn't seen much of anything, she'd been in such an all-fired rush to get out of there. What a crappy detective she'd be. And what a scaredy-cat! Every little rustle of leaf or creak of branch made her start. A tree trunk scraping against another made a noise like someone crying, which is what she felt like doing.

The path took her past an old shack that leaned to one side back of the Johnsons' cabin. And then the lake appeared, glimmering, beyond the trees.

Francie found the trail that led to her aunts' cabin and was just headed in that direction when she stopped. Down by the lake, on the dock, was the unmistakable outline of a person. Someone was kneeling at the end of the dock with his hands in the water. Theo.

She had her mouth open to holler at him when she realized what he was doing. He was washing his hands.

Blood rushed to her head and rang in her ears, loud as any school bell. After what she'd seen in Digby's tent, it gave her the chills watching him. She ran. She ran and ran until she ran right into her aunts' cabin.

The new sheriff, when she arrived at the cabin, was as unlike the previous sheriff as a person could be. For one thing, she was a woman. And she was young. And she was taking this death very seriously. "Suspected foul play," Sheriff Warner said, after she had inspected the body, but she wouldn't say more until after the autopsy results were in.

When Francie was escorted into the back bedroom to be interviewed, the sheriff turned a pair of sharp eyes on her and said, "You found the body?"

Francie nodded and said that she had gone to find Digby (leaving out that she'd actually been looking for Theo) and she did find him, but he was dead.

"Did you touch anything?"

"No," Francie said, peeling a leaf off the bottom of her shoe. "I came back here, told my aunts, and they called your office."

"When was the last time you saw Professor Digby alive?"

"Earlier this evening."

Now the sheriff looked up. "Oh?" she said.

"There was a kind of field trip from school. I guess Digby was supposed to meet them at the dock, but he didn't show up, so I walked the group back to the site. I saw Digby then."

"Who was this field trip group composed of?"

Francie resisted the impulse to correct the detective's sentence structure and answered, "Theater students from the high school and their teacher, or director, I guess, Mr. Redburn."

"Do you know the other students?"

"I only know the first names of two of the students," Francie answered. "It was my first day of school."

"That's all right. I can get the list from Keith," the sheriff said. Hastily correcting herself, she added, "Mr. Redburn."

Francie couldn't avoid raising her eyebrows. Keith? So the sheriff and the theater director were on a first-name basis. It probably didn't mean diddly-squat, she thought. Small town, after all.

"Did Digby say anything about finding something else out there?" the sheriff asked.

"Something else?" Francie said. "Like what?"

"I don't know. He sent a message just today that I should stop out at the site, that he had found something I might find interesting."

Francie shook her head. "He wouldn't have told *me*, anyway," she said. "That's for sure."

"Okay," the sheriff said, standing and stretching her back. "That's all for now. If you remember anything, any little detail, even if it seems insignificant, give me a call."

"Sure," Francie got up and started for the door.

"But," the sheriff said, her tone changing, and Francie felt her stomach flip as she turned back. "There's one more thing," she went on. "I know you did some sleuthing out here this summer."

Francie didn't respond, except to look at Sheriff Warner, wondering where this was going.

"I just want to remind you that Rydell Johnson is no longer the sheriff of this county," the new sheriff said. "I am. And I'm telling you: don't try any Nancy Drew stuff with this investigation."

Francie felt her blood, if not boil, at least start simmering. A comment like that just made her want to start investigating right that instant, but she tamped down her anger and tried to keep her voice light as she said, "Don't worry! Not interested. Busy with school and everything."

After the sheriff and deputies left, Francie and Theo sat eating the cold dinner that had been meant to be shared with Digby. The aunts fluttered nearby, fetching the salt and pepper, a napkin, a glass of water.

"My goodness!" Astrid said. "Digby murdered! Think of it. Isn't it exciting?"

Francie mumbled something noncommittal with her mouth full of stroganoff. Fatigue coupled with the drama of the past few hours had plunged her into a kind of loopy exhaustion.

"Who do you think did it?" Jeannette posed the question to everyone. "Could have been anyone. Everyone disliked him. If I was Evelyn Smattering, I'd have stabbed him a hundred times over!"

Theo guffawed so hard he started choking.

"Theo?" Astrid said. "Are you quite all right? Didn't anyone ever tell you not to laugh with your mouth full?"

"Sorry," Theo said. "But why would nice old Mrs. Smattering want to kill Digby?"

"Well, Evelyn was such a thoughtful hostess and so solicitous, and then he was such a boor!" Astrid said.

"He'd scold her if the coffee wasn't hot enough," Jeannette added, "or if she didn't make it fast enough. And then, without a word, he moved out and just lived at the site in that tent of his. Honestly! Quite a horrible man. Right, Francie?"

"Yup." Francie glanced at Theo to see his reaction. None.

"Maybe he wasn't horrible to everyone," Jeannette said. "Even though it seemed like nobody liked him!"

"I know one person who didn't hate him," Francie said. "Mr. Redburn, the theater director. I guess they went to school together, and Redburn seemed to idolize the guy. I think he brought his theater club out here to impress them with his connections. At least that's what one of the students told me."

"Hmm," Theo murmured.

"Did you know him?" Francie blurted.

Theo glanced at her, guzzled the last of a glass of milk, and said, "Not really." That was it.

In that case, she knew she should ask him why he and Digby had been arguing, but she was so surprised that he didn't offer to explain himself that she couldn't think of what to say.

"It must have been someone on the dig, I suppose," Astrid mused, absently stirring the creamed onions. "The cook was done for the season, so the two girls, Mallory and Gretchen, would have been at Mrs. Hansen's, and the two boys, Jackson and . . . and . . . the other one, would have been at Potter's, I suppose."

"Maybe it was the pipeline people," Jeannette said. "Digby raised a ruckus with some guy with the energy company about the damage to potential archaeological sites. He was on the side of the tribe who said the bulldozers had already plowed over burial sites. I guess there was one good thing about him."

"Well, it's so exciting!" Astrid said. "Another mystery to solve! Right, Francie?"

"Nope," Francie said firmly. "Not interested." She noticed the aunts giving each other a *look*, so she knew she'd have to explain herself. "I won't have any extra time to solve mysteries because . . ." Then realizing she'd have to give them some reason for her reluctance, she added impulsively, "I'm going to audition for the school play."

Theo gave her a sideways glance, eyebrows cocked at a skeptical angle.

The aunts, however, cooed over this, happy that things were going so well at school already. Francie wasn't so sure about that, but she didn't want to go anywhere near this investigation. It wasn't the sheriff warning her off—that was a challenge to which she'd willingly rise. It was the memory of Theo washing his hands in the lake. She supposed she could just ask him what he'd been doing, but he should explain himself without being asked, shouldn't he? And anyway, she wasn't sure she wanted to know the answer. What was it he'd said? "Sometimes it's better not to know."

So now, she supposed, she'd have to audition for that play.

6
AUDITIONS

I T   W A S N ' T   U N T I L   S H E   W A S   W A I T I N G for her turn to audition
that it really hit her. Sitting in the darkened auditorium, with
the drone of students reading lines on the lighted stage, she
was struck by the realization: her brother could be a murderer.
Was it possible? Theo? Her own brother? But she didn't really
know him. He'd been out of her life for nearly three years, and
who knew what he'd been doing all that time?

Something was going on with him—that was obvious. She
retraced what had happened the night he'd turned up. He'd
shown up at her apartment late at night, peeked out the window,
then dragged her through town until they ended up breaking
into Muskie Bait. Where had he learned how to pick a lock, she
wondered, and why were they chased by somebody in a trench
coat, someone she'd knocked out with a can of maple syrup,
which was, by anybody's standards, ridiculous?

The weirdest part of it was that there had been no repercus-
sions. There'd been no mention of it in the news, no police ques-

tioning, only a comment by a girl in English class. How strange was that? In one way, Francie would like to ask Theo all this stuff, but in another way, maybe she didn't want to know. So she was trying her hardest to avoid him right now.

Francie looked up in time to see a girl from the field trip—she recognized her as the tall blonde who'd volunteered at the dig site that summer—begin reading the part of Antigone. She was putting a lot into it.

"I think I could really do a good job with this part, Mr. Redburn," the girl said after he cut her off.

"Uh-huh," he said.

"I mean, I feel like it's kind of made for me."

"Okay, Phoebe," he said. "I'll take everything into consideration."

The next actor stepped up onto the stage and Francie drifted back to her dilemma. On top of everything else there was the issue that she had wondered long and hard about: her mother. Who had she been and why wouldn't anyone tell her anything about her? It had certainly occurred to Francie that perhaps the reason was that her mother had done some unspeakable thing—murder, for instance. So it wasn't an enormous leap to imagine that her son might have followed in her footsteps.

Francie heard her name called and she walked onto the stage, opened to the page mentioned, and let the whirlwind in her mind go silent while she immersed herself in the words of the play. Even though they had been written more than two thousand years ago, these lines still resonated with universal human grief and suffering.

"They say that he's to be left unburied and unwept," she began, reading the part of Antigone speaking of her slain brother. "His body must lie in the fields, a sweet treasure for birds to feed on to their heart's content. That is what they say, and the noble Creon is coming to proclaim it publicly and the penalty—stoning to death in the public square!" Francie lost herself in the rhythm and cadence of the lines, the rise and fall of sound, but when she came to the lines "And now you can prove what you are: a true sister, or a traitor to your family," she could barely get through them.

There was silence when she finished.

"Very nice," Mr. Redburn said. "You put a lot of emotion into that."

Francie nodded and returned to her seat, aware that all eyes followed her.

She tuned out as the other kids read for parts. Her mind was on her own dilemma, which, when you boiled it down, was what did it mean to be a true sister? To protect your brother at all costs? Or did she have an obligation to reveal what she'd seen and heard? Should she confront Theo? What would she say? *Did you kill Digby?* She could hardly bring herself to *think* those words, much less say them. And what if he said yes? What would she do then? Would she turn in her own brother?

And what if he said no? That might just mean he was a liar, which he had already admitted to her that he was, and not hard to imagine if a person was also a murderer. On the dock at the cabin he'd talked about having to lie his whole life, then he'd said, "It's not good to lie that much." What had that meant?

Just who was this brother who knew how to break into buildings and who had been chased by Mr. Trench Coat for who knew what reason? Was Theo in danger? Or was *Theo* the danger?

Auditions must have ended, Francie realized, because the other students were filing out of the room. She got up and was walking out, too, when her name was called, and she turned back to see Mr. Redburn motioning her to come down to the front of the hall. Others glanced back, but it seemed she was the only one being called. Maybe he meant to tell her there wouldn't be a part for her? Whatever. She could think up some other excuse to not have time to do any sleuthing.

As she walked down the aisle, the girl named Phoebe passed her and shot her a poisonous glance. Oh boy, Francie thought, I've already made an enemy.

"I'm giving you the part of Antigone," Mr. Redburn said.

"What?" Francie squeaked. "Maybe you haven't read my audition form yet—where I said that I only wanted a small part."

"That may be what you thought, but we need someone experienced to play Antigone."

"What makes you think I have any experience?"

He tilted his head and gave her a look. "I know about your acting career," he said.

Sheesh! Francie thought. He Googled me? How else would he know about her acting background, that she'd been in a short-lived TV show in which she played a kid detective, had some bit parts in things in New York, and had attended an arts high school in Brooklyn?

"I also know that you have a reputation as a detective," he went on, "but I hope you don't intend to get involved with that business out at Enchantment." Before Francie could protest that she had no interest, he continued, "I need you to focus all your energy on this part. It's a lot of lines to learn and you have to be a good role model for the rest of the cast. They don't have your level of experience."

"I'm really sorry, but maybe it would be best if you gave the part to Phoebe," Francie said. "I think she really wants it."

"No," he said. "Phoebe doesn't have the . . ." He seemed to search for a diplomatic way of putting it. "The *gravitas* that you have. The maturity."

He meant that Francie looked older than Phoebe. Francie was

familiar with people thinking she was older than she really was, in part because of the white streak in her hair. But apparently there was also gravitas, whatever that was.

"Or Raven," Francie said. "What about Raven?"

"No, she always works on tech. She's an excellent lighting designer and always runs the lights."

"Maybe she'd like a shot at a part," Francie said.

"Excuse me," Mr. Redburn said. "Who is the director here? Are you in the habit of casting other people's plays?"

Well, Francie thought, she'd wanted an excuse to stay away from the investigation, and getting the lead in the school play was probably about as good an excuse as there was. It would mean she'd have rehearsals after school or evenings and probably some weekends, too. It would give her a way to avoid Theo, the sheriff, and the whole "business out at Enchantment." So she said, "Okay."

7

RICING

Hoping to avoid Theo over the weekend, Francie made plans to go harvesting wild rice with Raven. Saturday morning she was waiting outside for Raven when her phone dinged. Text from Theo:

> What are you doing today?
>
> > Ricing with Raven.
>
> Where?
>
> > All I know is not on the
> > rez. That's how come I
> > can go along, I guess.
> > Otherwise you have
> > to be a member of the
> > band.
>
> Got any theories on the
> murder?
>
> > No.

Weren't you the one who
solved all the murders last
summer?

More credit than I
deserved.

Aren't you even the slightest
bit interested?

Don't have time bc I got the
lead in the play.

"I thought you said you didn't want the lead," a voice behind her said.

She spun around to see Theo standing there. "What are you doing in town?" she asked.

"Came to see you!" he said brightly. "Now what about this role in the play?"

"I told the director I didn't want it," Francie said, "but he insisted."

"I suppose you could have said no," Theo said. "Weren't you worried about making enemies of the girl who always wanted the big part, and all that stuff you said?"

"I guess I caved."

"Well, it'll be a good way to meet people."

"Uh-huh."

"But anyway, it doesn't preclude you from having an opinion on this murder."

"I don't know anything!" Francie said. "Everybody seemed to despise Digby, so . . ." Now would be a good time to bring up his argument with Digby, she knew. She should ask Theo what he'd been doing when she saw him at the lake. The longer she waited to mention it, the harder it would be to bring it up. But then, she thought, why didn't *he* bring it up? Why didn't he explain himself?

"Why are you here, Theo?" Francie blurted out.

"I told you—I came into town to see you. Hoped we could hang out a little."

"I mean, why are you here at all?"

"I was worried about you," he said. "All those murders—you were in danger!"

"Well, you're a bit late now. That was two months ago!"

"Travel is slow by yak."

"Yak?"

"I was in Mongolia."

"They don't have the internal combustion engine there?"

"Not where I was."

"Okay, well, I'm fine," Francie said. "As you can see."

Something was fishy about this. She'd like to think he'd come yak-trekking to her rescue, but she didn't believe it. Something else was going on. What? Right now, she just wanted to slug him. While she had to go to school, keep her grades up, and get into a good college, Theo was tapping into his trust fund and gallivanting all over the world having adventures.

"To tell you the truth, Theo, I feel like I have a lot of questions about you," she said.

"Oh, you mean the Muskie Bait episode?" he asked.

"For starters."

"Yeah, I owe you an explanation about that. And, I suppose you want to know about Mom. I actually came here in part because I realized it was time you knew the whole story," Theo said. "Or as much of it as I know."

Francie's breath caught somewhere before it reached her lungs. She actually could not breathe for what seemed like a full minute. She heard herself saying the words, "Yes! It's about time!" while part of her was thinking, Maybe I don't really want to know.

Francie was saved from knowing anything because Raven drove up in her mom's car, jumped out, and said, "Hi, Francie. Hi, Francie's brother." She held out her hand to Theo, who shook it.

"You must be Raven," Theo said, still holding on to her hand. "I'm Theo, but you can call me 'Frenchy's brother' if you prefer."

"Frenchy, huh?" Raven smiled at Francie. "Nice to meet you, then, Theo-Frenchy's-brother." Francie noticed they were still shaking hands.

Geez! Francie thought. Did Raven's face just get prettier, her hair glossier, her eyes more exotic? And Theo! His face had taken on a kind of movie star glow, too. Francie stared at Raven, then Theo, then back at Raven again. Some kind of wizardry had just taken place that she did not understand.

"Well, we better get going!" Francie said, suddenly worried that Raven would invite Theo along for the day.

"Do you want to come along?" Raven asked Theo. "We might be able to find you a spot in a canoe."

Theo glanced at Francie, then said vaguely, "Oh, I've got plans."

"Maybe next time," Raven said.

Francie quickly realized why Raven had insisted that she wear long pants and a long-sleeved shirt. Not just because of sun, but because the rice had sharp barbs that pricked. Also there were little biting worms involved.

It was hard work, too, whether standing in the back of the canoe, poling through the tall stalks of rice (actually a kind of grass, Raven explained), or sitting in the bow, bending the stalks over the canoe with a smooth wooden stick called a rice knocker, and smacking them with another knocker to make the kernels fall off the stalks and into the bottom of the canoe. There they collected in a nice heap of musky smelling, fall-colored grains, some miscellaneous foliage, and also bugs and worms.

It was a still day on the marshy river, and there were a few other canoes out, some of them filled with Raven's relatives. For a while, Francie, who was working the rice knockers, could hear the murmur of conversation coming from the other canoes. After a time they all seemed to disperse, disappearing among the reeds, and it seemed as if she and Raven were the only people on Earth. Except for a few flies, lazily buzzing, and the thrum of a hummingbird chasing a red-winged blackbird, it was quiet. There was just the sound of the rice hissing along the side of the boat, the rustle of the stalks being bent over the canoe, and the *chik-chik* of the knockers.

"My grandma used to be my ricing partner," Raven said. "Then my mom tried it. But she hates the worms and bugs and stuff."

"Well," Francie said, picking a few off her clothes and dropping them into the water. "They are pretty gross."

"Yeah, but look at all the good rice we're getting!" Raven exclaimed.

The canoe began to look like it was growing hair or fur. Dozens of tiny white spiders emerged and immediately got to work climbing their invisible threads, so they seemed to be suspended in midair.

"What about *your* mom?" Raven said. "Is she the ricing type?"

The canoe moved out into the open pond where the clouds appeared to float in the water, and Francie felt as if, spiderlike, she was afloat somewhere between lake and sky. It was a familiar feeling—that of not belonging anywhere, of being adrift—

largely because she didn't know anything about her mother, she supposed.

"I don't know if she would have been. She died when I was a baby," Francie said, telling Raven the story she herself had been told yet had never believed. "And my dad died in a car accident seven years ago." At least she knew her dad had died in a car crash. Whether it was an accident or not was up for debate. At least in her mind.

"Gosh!" Raven said. "I'm sorry. That's tough."

To get off the subject, Francie pointed at a likely looking patch of rice and said, "What do you think about that spot? Do you think we can get the canoe in there?"

While Raven maneuvered them into the indicated rice bed, Francie thought again about how she might find out more about her mother. She did have one lead, one thing that she felt might hold an answer, or a clue, or something, and she was pretty sure she knew where that something was. Trouble was, she wasn't sure she was brave enough to go after it.

"So," Raven said, "I should explain that dumb jail comment from lunch the other day."

"That's okay," Francie said. "You don't have to."

"Those boys are just stupid. See, it was about a protest."

"You were protesting something?"

"The pipeline."

Oh yeah, Francie thought. "The pipeline carries . . . oil?" she ventured.

"Crude," Raven explained. "The really dirty stuff—375,000 gallons of it going through the pipeline *per day*. The planned route goes through a lot of environmentally sensitive streams and wetlands—and there aren't people around in these remote places. There could be a spill or leak for a long time before anybody would even know. Only 20 percent of spills are discovered by the company. Most are found by landowners or just . . . people, people who can't do anything about it. So if—or maybe I should say *when*—it leaks or there's an accident, that'd be dirty crude oil going right into the watershed, the watershed that's part of Enchantment Lake, you know. It'd put an end to the rice, too."

"Well, that stinks," Francie said.

"Yeah, it literally stinks," Raven agreed. "How do you not know about this?"

"Sorry!" Francie said. "I spent the summer at my aunts' cabin. No TV, Internet, not even electricity. So I'm a little uninformed."

They quit talking for a bit. The rice was thick in this spot and Raven pushed the canoe through the bed pretty fast, so Francie had to work to keep up.

Finally, Raven said, "How's the investigation going?"

"What investigation?" Francie said, distractedly.

"Is there more than one?"

"Oh, you mean the murder."

"Uh . . . yeah?" Raven said.

"You probably know more than me. I mean, your dad's a cop, right?"

"On the rez!" Raven said. "He doesn't have anything to do with the Enchantment murder." She paused to shove the canoe deeper into the rice. "What do *you* think? Maybe that girl we heard Digby insulting—Mallory—maybe she did it? Or those other college intern types? They all seemed to hate the guy."

"Uh-huh," Francie said, trying to sound bored. Maybe Raven would take the hint and change the subject.

"Hey!" Raven said. "Maybe it was the pipeline guy. The one Digby went all ballistic on because his bulldozers were wrecking potential archaeological spots. They're saying there was a mystery person out at the dig site the day of the murder. Maybe it was the pipeline guy."

Francie stopped whacking rice. "Mystery person?" she asked.

"Yeah, I guess there was some guy there that nobody had ever seen before. He talked to Dr. Digby in his tent, and then nobody saw any more of him."

Francie sat up and took in a big lungful of air. The drying reeds and grasses, the musky rice, the marshy water all seemed to smell like hope for a moment. But then she realized the mystery person must be Theo, and the marsh smelled like muck again. No one at the site would have known who Theo was. And she knew he'd been there. So the mystery person must be him.

Raven rattled on about possible motives, while Francie's mind drifted, wondering what her brother's motive could be. She came back to the conversation in time to hear Raven saying, "Don't you have some kind of a theory lurking somewhere?"

"No."

"You're so boring!" Raven joked. "I thought you'd be like hanging out with Nancy Drew."

Francie groaned. "If I hear myself associated with her one more time, I'm going to burn all the Nancy Drew books in the library."

"You can't," Raven said. "I checked them all out in seventh grade and still haven't returned them."

Francie laughed and said, having a sudden thought, "I'll tell you what—you want some Nancy Drew action? I've got some."

"Yeah?" Raven said.

"Are you in?" Francie asked.

Raven emitted a little squeak of excitement and breathed out the word, "Totally."

8

THE SILVER BOX

THE POLICE TAPE had been removed and the huge summer home was empty. Francie remembered how it had been all lit up and looked like a cruise ship run aground when she'd attended a party there in the summer. Now it was empty and forlorn, leaves had collected on the many decks, and cobwebs clung to walls and drain spouts.

The once immaculate sweep of yard now looked like a hay-field, and Francie and Raven had to wade through it to get to the front steps of the house. Beyond the house, the lake clung to the last of the daylight, emanating a soft glow.

Francie shoved aside a layer of moldering leaves with her foot as she stepped onto the deck.

"You're sure there's nobody here?" Raven whispered, following behind Francie.

"The person who owns it is in jail," Francie answered, jiggling the door handle. It was locked, and she moved along the deck to another door.

"Won't all the doors be locked?" Raven asked.

"Yeah, probably."

Nonetheless, Francie checked the many doors while Raven scanned the woods that ringed the property.

"You know there is a still-unsolved murder that happened out here, right? You know that, right?" Raven trailed Francie as she circled the house looking for an open door. "Well, all the doors are locked," Raven said. "I guess we have to give up."

Francie produced a credit card and slid it between door and frame until the lock clicked open.

"Ooh boy," Raven said. "Where'd you learn that trick?"

"I learned it from my brother."

"Theo? Where did he learn it?"

"I don't know, and I'm not sure I want to find out."

The place was stuffy, with that closed-up smell and a faint scent of something sort of sweet, a strange odor Francie couldn't quite place. Rather than switching the lights on, the girls opted for flashlights and roamed from room to room, the beams bouncing over furniture, lamps, artwork, momentarily illuminating the black eyes of a moose head on a wall and the beady eyes of a bear rug on the floor.

"This place has more eyes than a sack of potatoes," Raven said and shone her flashlight on Francie. "Are you sure you want to do this?" she asked. "You look kind of pale."

"I'm fine," Francie said, although a familiar cold tremor ran through her. Her fingers were suddenly cold and stiff, and her chest throbbed.

"Tell me what we're looking for again," Raven whispered.

"A small silver box," Francie choked out. Her throat felt thick with something. She didn't think coming back to this house would affect her, but she had to admit that her nerves were jangled. "Um," she continued, trying to stay focused, "I saw it here last summer. But I remember one just like it from when I was little. It belonged to my mother."

"Okay . . . ," Raven said. "What does this have to do with the murder?"

"Nothing, as far as I know."

"Wait. What? Why are we here?"

"It's something I really want to find," Francie said. "The box disappeared at some point when I was little. And then I saw it here last summer. I've never seen another one like it and I . . . I don't know, I just want to look at it, that's all!"

"How big is it?" Raven asked.

"Maybe about the size of a pound of butter," Francie said. At least that's how she remembered it. Was it? She really couldn't say for sure. "It's not in here," Francie said, moving to the next room. Think! she told herself. You saw it, then things happened and you got distracted. But you saw it.

She stopped to picture the scene as she remembered it when she had seen it in this house. It had been so unexpected, yet there it was, exactly as she had pictured it in the years following its disappearance, ornately engraved and gleaming: the silver box. Maybe it was just a fanciful invention of her imagination. But then she had seen it—a real thing—and it had been here! Hadn't it?

Even now, just thinking of it brought on an almost memory of her mother—a shred, a wisp, like a nearly remembered dream . . . She strove for it, but it eluded her, dissolving like mist. Oh, if there were only something she could remember! There was so much not knowing in her life. Who was her mother? Why had she disappeared? *Why would no one tell her anything about her?*

If she could lay her hands on that box, though, Francie felt certain it would answer a lot of questions. And there was something else: even though she knew it was irrational, she had always imagined that her heart was inside the box. There was a fairy tale she'd heard as a kid about a troll who had no heart in his body. Far, far away in a lake was an island, so the tale went. And on that island stood a church; in that church was a well, in that well swam a duck, in that duck was an egg, and in that egg lay the troll's heart.

In her story, it would go: *Far, far away, there is a lake, and near the lake stands a house; in the house there is a table; on the table sits a box; in the box there lies my heart.*

"You are seriously creeping me out right now," Raven said. "You've been shining your flashlight on that table for about five minutes, and anyone can see there is nothing on it!"

Francie snapped out of her reverie and swept the beam over the room. "I'm sure that's where it was." She let her light come to rest once again on the same end table.

"Maybe the police took the box as evidence," Raven whispered.

"Why would they?" Francie whispered back. "And why are we whispering?"

"I don't know," Raven answered, "but it feels like we're not alone."

As soon as Raven said it, Francie felt it. The hairs on her arms and the back of her neck prickled.

Someone else was inside the house.

"Come on!" Francie whispered, moving toward the sound of footsteps.

"Are you insane?" Raven whispered back. "We should be running *away*. It might be *the* murderer!" She tugged on Francie's arm, but Francie plunged into the hall, dragging Raven along with her.

"There!" she whispered, catching a glimpse of someone disappearing through an open door: a leg, a foot, one arm, a hand, and clutched in the hand—had she imagined it, or had she seen just the faintest flash of silver?

As soon as the door clicked shut, Francie turned to Raven. "I think he's got it. We have to go after him." She charged down the hall toward the door.

"No!" Raven cried, running after her.

Francie already had her hand on the doorknob when Raven reached her and yanked her away.

"Think!" she said. "If you go out there, whoever it is will see you!"

"If I don't go out there, I won't see whoever it is." Francie tore away from Raven, flung open the door, and charged out onto the deck in time to see the fleeing figure headed toward a boat on the beach. How had she not noticed that boat earlier?

"That's him, getting into a boat!" Francie cried. She raced across the expanse of lawn while the mystery person started the motor and plunged away from the shore.

Francie watched helplessly as the boat headed across the lake. Just before it receded into the gloom, the motor slowed, the driver reached down as if picking something off the bottom of the boat. Then he stood, and with an overhand motion sent the thing soaring into the air. There was a faint splash, stillness (during which Francie realized she was holding her breath), and then the motor roared back to life and the boat disappeared into the darkness.

9
FROM PLAY PRACTICE
TO PROTEST

THE NEXT DAYS were beautiful, quiet days when the water was probably like glass. Francie wouldn't know. She was stuck in the auditorium at play practice, imagining how perfect it would have been to be out on the lake in a boat looking down into the clear water, the canoe gliding over lacy weeds, stretches of sand peppered with snail shells, and here and there the forlorn skeleton of a crayfish.

She imagined the bright sheen on the water, the changing colors of the trees reflected on its surface, and the fallen leaves bright as gold coins in the shallow water. She imagined paddling a canoe straight out to the spot where she'd seen the box splash into the lake, and imagined seeing it gleaming underwater. Imagined diving in and scooping it up in her hand and—

"Francie?"

Francie looked up to see Mr. Redburn staring down at her from the stage. "What do you think?" he asked.

Francie hesitated, then cautiously asked, "About what?"

"Was it right or wrong for Antigone to do what she did? She broke the law, but was it morally right? And, if it's morally right, is it okay to break the law? Is it even our *obligation* to stand up for what we believe?"

"Which of those questions am I supposed to answer?" Francie squeaked.

Everybody laughed and Mr. Redburn said, "Let's all just think about those questions for the time being." He went on talking about the play, and Francie tried to stay focused but felt her mind drifting again. When she tuned back in, he was saying, "In theater, as in life, things are not always what they seem." Then he announced that Jay had prepared a report on the background of the play.

"Antigone had a totally messed-up family," Jay said. "Her father, Oedipus, married his own mother, and when he found out what he'd done, he gouged out his own eyes. His wife-and-mother, Jocasta, killed herself."

"Is Jay doing this for a class or something?" Francie whispered to Raven.

"No," Raven said. "He just likes to do research. It's his thing. Everybody's got to have a 'thing,' right?"

"I guess," Francie said. Looking around, she saw that the rest of the cast and crew were dozing in their seats. Phoebe glanced up, smirked at Francie, then went back to her phone. Phoebe had volunteered at the dig site this summer. Could she have been the killer?

Francie forced herself to turn her attention to Jay's speech. He had already gotten through the whole story of Antigone's brothers going to war against each other.

"It was agreed to let the matter be decided by brother-to-brother combat," Jay was saying. "And what happened was, the two brothers ended up killing each other. Antigone decides she's going to bury her brother, which is when the play starts, and her punishment is to be shut up in a tomb to die. Afterwards, her sister Ismene sort of disappears, and that is the end of the house of Oedipus. The last of the royal family of Thebes was known no more. The end."

Messed-up family, Francie thought, like mine. Maybe Francie's family wasn't *that* messed up, but they could be. That was the thing—she didn't really know. Her brother might be a murderer. Her mother was—what?—she didn't know. Francie didn't even know if her mother was alive or dead. And the only way to find out anything about her was to find a box on the bottom of a pretty big body of water, or talk to Theo, the person she most wanted to avoid.

On Saturday, instead of going to look for the silver box, Francie drove with Raven to a protest.

"We're not going to get arrested, are we?" Francie gripped the steering wheel with both hands as she steered the car down the gravel road. She didn't feel sure about her decision to go to a protest with Raven, but it was so windy that trying to find anything on the bottom of a lake would be a hopeless endeavor.

"Arrested? No!" Raven said. "Why? Oh, those stupid boys? Did you think I really was in jail?" She laughed. "Just a bunch of us protesters were taken to the police station one time. They let us go. We were never in jail or anything."

"Why did they take you in?"

"Beats me," Raven said. "For our own safety, is what Sheriff Johnson said."

"Oh, yeah, him," Francie said sourly. "Rydell. I know him."

"Hey, slow down." Raven peered out the passenger-side window. "There they are!"

"Where?"

"On the other side of that field."

"How do we get there?"

"It's a long way around, especially since the road ahead is blocked. And turning around the other way will really take a long time. We'll miss the speaker if we go that way. Just park here and we'll cut through the field."

Francie pulled the car over and shut off the engine. The girls gathered their backpacks and the signs they'd made that morning in Francie's apartment and got out of the car. The wind whipped their hair in their faces and tried to tear the signs out of their hands, but they forged on, holding the barbed wire fence for each other, then starting across the field of stubble.

"One thing you might not have known about Professor Digby is that he wasn't a total jerk," Raven explained as they picked their way through the field. With the wind in their ears, it was hard to hear, so Raven had to shout. "The tribe has been concerned about some places that may contain ancestral remains, and Digby was standing up to the energy company about that."

"Yeah, I kinda heard about it." Francie looked across the field. Quite a distance away, she could see a gathering of people. Television crews were there, too, by the look of the vans with satellites affixed to their roofs. When the wind died, she caught snatches of sound from the protest: a voice on a loudspeaker, amplified music, a strange rumbling growl coming from somewhere, and Raven's voice, saying, ". . . something kind of interesting about those bones."

"What bones?" Francie shouted.

"The bones! The bones out at Enchantment. That you found!"

"I didn't find them."

"Well, whatever. What if someone was trying to steal them?

Maybe somebody was busy stealing bones when Digby confronted them and they had to kill him?"

"Why would anybody want to steal mastodon bones?" Francie asked.

"Well, I've been thinking, and it's possible. See, my grandma is Dakota—"

"You mean she's from North Dakota?"

Raven let out a little exasperated sigh, then put on her patient voice and said, "No. She *is* Dakota. It's a tribe. Like Ojibwe."

"Okay."

The field of stubble had given way to dirt that looked like it had been churned up by machines with wide tires. Francie kept her eyes down, trying not to step into mud puddles, while Raven went on. "So she told me that in Dakota stories there's this ancient being, a kind of enormous water monster called Unktehi that lived long, long ago. Huge, you know. With big horns that went to the sky. Its body could swell to cause floods. But it died out long, long ago. Still, sometimes its bones were found and were prized for their *wakan*. The people collected the pieces of the bones for their medicine bags. Medicine men chewed on the bones as part of their initiation."

"That's interesting," Francie said. "But the bones they dug up at Enchantment are mastodon bones, not . . . um—"

"Unktehi," Raven said. "Paleontologists think the bones the medicine men found were probably mastodon or mammoth bones. It makes sense because back in those olden times, the people would have found these big bones, and they had to make sense of them, just like we do now."

"Okay, but I can't see how it would have any bearing in this case."

"What if there are still people wanting those bones, maybe even believing that they are the bones of Unktehi— some people believe in them, you know."

"As far as theories go, you have to admit that is pretty far out—"

"That's him! That's him!" Raven shouted.

"That's who?" Francie looked up to see two men in work clothes and hard hats striding toward them, each from a different direction.

"That one guy on the right is the power company guy that Digby had it out with!" Raven said. "I don't know who the other guy is. But he looks mad."

The man on the right waved his arms over his head; his mouth was moving as if he were shouting, but there was so much other noise between the wind, the music at the protest, and the sound of heavy machinery that Francie couldn't hear what he said. Her eyes flicked from him to the other man who was clearly shouting and whose face grew redder and redder and his gesticulating more alarming with every moment. By the time Francie realized that he was pointing at something behind them, it was too late. The hard ground gave way to a yawning chasm. As she fell into it, Francie realized, also too late, what was making the rumbling growl.

10
THE ER

WHAT WAS IT, Francie wondered, as she lay on the examining table, about her and bulldozers? There had been an episode with a bulldozer the past summer, too, and that made her think of the silver box and wonder why someone had stolen it. And why had that person thrown it into the lake, of all places? And why wasn't she at Enchantment right now looking for it instead of where she was, which was the ER, getting her head stitched up?

Half her face felt very numb, like she'd gotten way too much novocaine at the dentist's. When the nurse helped her stand, she felt like her legs might buckle under her. But she wobbled back to the waiting room. There was Raven, her ankle wrapped in an Ace bandage. Also waiting, unfortunately, was the sheriff.

"Did you want to press charges?" the sheriff asked.

"You mean we can press charges? Like for reckless endangerment or something?" Francie said.

"I wasn't talking to you," Sheriff Warner explained. "I was talking to Mr. Waxwing." She gestured toward the doorway, where the two men she'd seen just before she and Raven fell into the trench were standing. One of them, still red-faced and angry looking, the other one looking uncomfortable, his hard hat clenched in his hands.

"Darn right we're pressing charges!" the red-faced one said, while the other one said, "Now, Dale, they're just kids . . ."

Francie felt woozy and, just before she fainted, she caught only some of the sheriff's words—"trespassing . . . tampering with a pipeline . . . felony offense . . ."

The first thing she saw when she came to was the sheriff's face, a few inches away from her own. "Are you able to answer a few questions?"

Francie nodded. Looking around, she saw she was in some kind of conference room, and she and the sheriff were the only ones in it. She had no recollection of how she'd gotten there.

"You seem to have a knack for being at the wrong place at the wrong time," the sheriff said.

Francie noticed a glass of water in front of her and took a long drink. Other than defending herself against charges of trespassing or whatever else she might be charged with, she planned to keep her mouth as firmly closed as possible.

"You girls were lucky that Mr. Waxwing was there, or you might have gotten hurt."

"Waxwing?"

"He may have saved your lives, or at least saved you from worse injuries."

"That's nice of him," Francie said. "On the other hand, if he hadn't been yelling at us, we probably would have seen that trench before we fell in it. Anyway, we weren't trying to do anything illegal. We were just trying to cut through that field to get to the rally."

"I get that," the sheriff said, surprising Francie. "You're also lucky that Mr. Waxwing didn't press charges. But just . . . be more careful, okay? And pay attention. And don't do that anymore."

Francie nodded. She was a little puzzled. She'd expected more trouble. Maybe the sheriff would just let her go and there wouldn't be anything on her record.

"Now," Sheriff Warner began, "about the investigation." It seemed the sheriff wasn't quite finished. "You seem to be avoiding anything having to do with it—Enchantment, your aunts, your brother . . ."

Francie's jaw dropped. "You told me not to get involved!"

"Sure," the sheriff said. "I guess I did. I didn't think you'd pay any attention to that, though." She looked down at a clipboard on the desk, so Francie couldn't tell what her expression was. Was she smiling? Or what?

Francie was wary. Maybe the sheriff was cagier than she let on. Francie would have to watch her step, she thought.

"Is there anything else you remember from the day of the murder? From the scene? Anything?"

Francie felt a little fuzzy. The anesthetic hadn't worn off, and she had a feeling she was slurring her words. Still, there was something. Francie remembered hearing someone arguing with Digby in his tent. She didn't know who it could have been because everyone except Digby was outside at the time. If she brought it up, though, the sheriff might assume it had been Theo, and since Francie couldn't identify who it was, she decided to keep that tidbit to herself.

"I didn't see anybody," Francie said, honestly.

The sheriff leaned back and plucked a large manila envelope out of her satchel. Then, as if performing a magic trick, she slowly pulled something out of a plastic bag. "Does this look familiar?" she asked, holding up a scarf.

"It's mine. Or very like one that I had."

"Had?"

Francie shrugged. "I guess I lost it."

"And when was that?"

The sheriff's pale blue eyes bored into Francie, who was remembering that she had tied Theo's hair back with that scarf the day of the murder. However, she did not intend to say so.

"Why do you ask?" Francie said, trying to go on the offensive.

"Any recollection of when you might have 'lost' the scarf?" the sheriff asked. Francie didn't like the way she said *lost*.

"I don't know," Francie said slowly. "Maybe I dropped it when I found the body." She hadn't, and she knew she hadn't, and she knew she was lying. It felt worse than a pinprick to her conscience—more like a little stab with a steak knife. "I had it that day—the day of the murder—but then I must have misplaced it. There were a lot of people around. Anybody could have picked it up." *Stab stab stab.*

"I suppose that's so," Sheriff Warner said. "You don't remember when you lost it?"

"I had it on the boat ride over . . ." Francie began, then paused. Would anyone remember that it had been in Theo's hair? "I suppose it might have blown into the lake." She remembered how Theo had said keeping a secret required constant lying—until it seemed like you were lying about everything. She was starting to understand what he meant. "Or maybe it fell off on the path," she added, weakly.

"This is not what your brother says."

"Oh?" Was she getting boxed into a corner?

"Your brother says that you gave it to him."

"I don't remember that," Francie said, guardedly.

"Would he be saying that to protect you?" the sheriff asked.

Francie's head jerked up. With a jolt, she realized what was going on here. She had been concentrating so hard on not pointing a finger at Theo that she hadn't realized that she herself was a suspect. Now she had to tread very carefully to extricate herself from suspicion while not implicating her brother.

"So, wait," she said. "Are you accusing me of murder?"

"I'm not accusing you of anything," Sheriff Warner said. "I am just following a line of inquiry. But, as I like to say, 'Where there's smoke, there's fire.'"

"Sometimes there's just smoke," Francie muttered.

"What?"

"Things are not always what they seem," Francie said, repeating Mr. Redburn's words, "in life as in theater."

The sheriff squinted at Francie as if trying to discern what that meant and then went on. "So," she continued, "at the time of the murder, you had opportunity, you had—" Here she held up the scarf. "—means . . ."

"Wait a minute," Francie said. "Are you saying my scarf is the murder weapon?"

"Strangulation seems to be the cause of death."

With my scarf, Francie thought, the scarf I gave Theo. She scrambled to think. "Motive?" she asked. "What possible motive do I have?"

The sheriff paged through her notebook, then paused on one of the pages. "A witness says you were seen arguing with the victim."

"Everybody argued with him!" Francie protested. "Or I should say he argued with everyone. It's almost the only way he ever communicated." Francie bet that pretty much everyone on the site had argued with or been scolded by Digby, so why would someone single out her petty argument among all the others? Who would *do* that?

She described the argument to the sheriff, explaining that

earlier that summer Digby had chased her away from the site, saying she didn't belong there. Francie had been so irritated that she'd lost her temper—Digby had that effect on people, she noted—and she had told him that if it hadn't been for her, there'd be no site and he wouldn't be there, which might, she had mused aloud with a raised voice, be better for everyone. Then she'd stalked off. "It was hardly a threat," Francie finished. At least she hadn't meant it as a threat, but now she could see how it could be perceived that way. "So am I your prime suspect?" Francie asked. "Or whatever they call it."

"We're not ruling anything out at the moment," the sheriff said.

Great, thought Francie, so now *both* Theo and I are suspects.

11
LATER THE SAME DAY

FRANCIE STOOD in front of the picture window, staring out at the foaming whitecaps on the lake. Big clouds, white as clean sheets, raced across the otherwise blue sky. Beautiful weather if you weren't hoping to find something on the bottom of a lake.

She and Raven had planned to spend the day out in the canoe looking for the box, but it had been windy, so they'd gone to the protest instead. And, now, here she was at the cabin anyway, with Raven and a headache—although the headache wasn't Raven's fault. Her aunts had fussed over all three of them, Francie, Raven, and even Theo, even though all he'd done was pick up the two girls from the hospital.

Now, their very late lunch was over and Raven was helping wash the dishes. Theo had gone outside to chop wood, and Francie stood by the window trying to get up the nerve to confront him. Well, she thought, if I can stare down a bulldozer, I can confront Theo. She would lay it on the line. She'd go out there and say, "Theo, did you murder Digby? Just tell me: yes or no. No beating around the bush." Then she'd stand with her arms folded across her chest until he answered her. Once he had, she would demand to know about their mother.

Raven was still in the kitchen, drying dishes and chatting with the aunts, so Francie stalked out of the house and stood in front of Theo, hands on hips.

"Here," Theo said. "Hold this." He nodded toward the log balanced on the chopping block as he hefted the ax over his shoulder.

Francie reached toward the log, then jerked her arm away. "Wait a minute. You want me to hold that log while you split it? You'll probably chop my arm off!"

"Well, you're not supposed to hang onto it *that* long!" Theo protested. "Just hold it so it doesn't fall off the block before I can take a swing at it."

"No!" Francie said.

Theo set a different log on its edge, one that balanced unaided, while reciting from a poem. "*The scent of fresh wood / is among the last things you will forget / when the veil falls.*" He brought the ax down on the log and, with a crisp *whack*, split it in two. Scooping up one of the halves, he put it to his nose and inhaled. "*The scent of fresh white wood / in the spring sap time / as though life itself walked by you, / with dew in its hair.*"

"Theo . . . ," Francie began.

"Hans Børli," Theo said.

"What?"

"That's whose poem that is."

"Ah." Francie felt her resolve dissipating, but she rallied. "Theo, would it be possible to have an actual conversation?"

Theo leaned on the ax handle and, regarding her, said, "Yes, sorry. I was just feeling so much wordless joy right then that I got carried away."

"Huh?"

"That's another Hans Børli line about cutting wood," he explained. *The smell of resin and fresh wood . . . such things can fill a man with wordless joy.*"

Francie crammed her sigh as full of exasperation as she could muster.

"Listen," Theo lowered his voice to a near whisper, "I know you want to know about Mom."

Francie was a little thrown. She had meant to confront him about the murder, but it was as if . . . as if . . . it didn't even occur to him that she would want to know his involvement! What did that mean? It could mean that he had nothing to do with it, so it wouldn't occur to him. Or he could be throwing her off on purpose.

Francie's desire to know about her mother was like a red-hot ember that never seemed to cool. She burned with the desire to know. And yet . . . and yet . . . sometimes it felt like the ember was too hot to touch. She sat down on the chopping block.

"First of all," Theo said. "If I tell you this, you have to know that you cannot give this information to anyone. Anyone! Including your friend in there." He pointed his chin at the cabin.

Francie glanced in that direction. She could see the top of Raven's head through the window and her arm reaching up to stack plates in the cupboard above the sink.

"All right," Theo said. "Sit down; you're going to need to sit down."

"I am sitting, Theo," Francie reminded him.

"Oh, yeah," he said. "Just seemed like the thing to say."

Francie thought she was prepared for anything: her mother was a criminal, a murderer, maybe she was dead. Still, her legs trembled so much that she had to stand up and shake them one at a time.

"Mom is . . . she's not dead," Theo said. "I'm pretty sure."

Francie felt like a box emptied of its contents. Like a body devoid of bones and veins. "If she's alive," Francie said, "why—I mean, why did she leave us? What was all that stuff about her being dead?"

"You didn't buy it anyway."

"True."

"Mom worked for a government agency that investigates antiquity theft. Her specialty was stolen artifacts," Theo explained. "Things stolen from archaeological sites or museums, and so on. She was involved in watching an international smuggling ring and was investigating when she disappeared. Well, what happened is she went underground."

"Now you are just making stuff up!" Francie watched Theo's green-flecked eyes for the wink she thought sure was coming. But no wink came. "And so . . . what happened?" she asked.

"As near as I can figure, she came by something extremely valuable," he said. "It fell into her possession somehow."

"Somehow?"

"She probably stole it," Theo explained, then brought the ax down on a log, splitting it cleanly in two. He bent over, picked up one of the pieces, and when he looked up, his gaze shifted over Francie's shoulder. "Oh, hi, Raven," he said.

Francie turned to see Raven limping out of the cabin.

"I better get going pretty soon or my mom is going to worry," Raven said.

Francie nodded. While Raven and Theo chatted, Francie turned her gaze to the tumultuous lake. She sometimes wondered what it would be like to have a mom who worried about her. In fact, she'd lived years of her life longing for that. And then more years, after her father had died, longing for a dad to worry about her. Now she was over it. Or at least that's what she told herself.

Anyway, her granddad worried about her—maybe too much—and her great-aunts, too. But her granddad was still living out east and her aunts would soon leave the lake for Arizona, and she'd be on her own until spring. Of course there was her brother—her brother the possible murderer, she thought.

She glanced back at him, still talking to Raven. They both looked at her, then Theo scribbled something on a piece of paper and gave it to Raven. His phone number? Maybe Francie should have joined the conversation, but she turned her attention back to the lake, watching as it turned blue to jade green, then gray as the sun passed under a cloud. It was a turbulence she felt inside, as if whitecaps churned within her. Wind roared in her head and she could think of little else but wind, waves, and under the waves, somewhere, the silver box, rolling, turning, tumbling.

12
WIND

THE WIND WOULD NOT STOP BLOWING. It blew with such ferocity it tore the leaves off trees and sent them scraping across the school parking lot. Loose papers were snatched out of hands and swirled away in the wind. Plastic bags billowed, sailed through the air, snagged in trees, and rattled there, as if shaking their fists at people. Francie wouldn't have been surprised to see small children go sailing by.

It hardly mattered. She didn't have time to go hunting for silver boxes or anything else, for that matter. Between school and the play, every square inch of her life was taken.

Right now it was homework. She was about to sit down at the little table in her kitchen and get started when the phone rang.

It was Theo. "We didn't quite finish that conversation out at the cabin," he said. "How about I take you out for dinner?"

Francie opened the fridge. Except for a jar of olives, some sour milk, and a couple of withered apples, it was empty. "I have leftovers," she said, shutting the door. "And I have to study for a test." She didn't want to talk to Theo, didn't want to know any more about her mother. Her mother was a thief who abandoned her family, and for all she knew, her brother was a murderer. That was enough bad news, thank you very much.

"You have to eat something," he said.

"I really need to study."

"How about Saturday?"

"I'm doing something with Raven."

"All day?"

"Yeah."

None of this was strictly true or even pretty true. In fact, Francie found herself stretching the truth a lot. And she was relieved when Theo finally ended the conversation and hung up.

She opened the fridge again, hoping some leftovers had somehow magically appeared. Maybe she should have accepted Theo's invitation, she thought as she stared at the emptiness. She shifted her search to the cupboard and took out a box of Cap'n Crunch. After shaking some cereal into a bowl, she stood leaning up against the counter, eating it with her fingers.

The phone rang again. It was her grandfather.

She set the bowl down, squeezed her eyes shut, and answered.

"I hear you nearly got arrested," was the first thing out of his mouth.

"Did not get arrested," she said. "It was all a misunderstanding."

"How's your head?"

Man! He heard everything! She touched the stitches on her forehead. Fortunately, it was mostly covered by the hank of hair that she never got around to cutting. "It's okay," she said.

Francie imagined her grandfather thoughtfully twirling his white mustache while gazing at Central Park from his Manhattan apartment.

"I hear you're in a play."

"Yep," she said.

She pictured him straightening his already straight back when he said, "Don't let it interfere with your studies. I expect you to keep your grades up."

"Yep."

"Is this the way they talk in Minnesota? 'Yep'? Have you forgotten how to say yes?"

"Yep," Francie said. She couldn't help it.

"I hope you're joking," her granddad said, but she thought she heard a little chuckle. Then he went on. "Why aren't you spending time with your brother? He's come all that way to spend time with you."

"I'm busy! If he wanted to see me, he should have come in the summer when I didn't have school."

"He was busy."

"Well?" Francie said. "Now I'm busy." This was sort of true, actually, but even if it hadn't been, she would have tried to avoid Theo.

"Are you investigating the murder?"

"What? No!" she said.

"Why not?"

"My grades? Etcetera?" Francie said. "All that stuff you just said?"

"Pfft! Investigating a murder will be far more educational than school, anyway."

Francie held her phone out and stared at it. Had she heard those words from her grandfather?

"The sheriff doesn't want me to," Francie explained. "She told me to stay away from it."

"She should be glad for your help," he said, and humphed.

Francie barely got out a "good-bye, talk to you later," she was so speechless.

"Okay, now for some chemistry," she said aloud but hadn't even cracked the book when the phone rang again. This time it was Nels. The sound of his voice was like a massage for her ears, she thought, sinking back in her chair and laughing at the analogy.

"What?" he said.

"Nothing."

As he talked about his classes and professors she pictured his sun-streaked hair and stormy-lake blue eyes. But as soon as he brought up the murder, she tried to cut the conversation short, telling him she wasn't interested.

"You? Not interested?" he said, suspicion creeping into his voice.

"I don't have time," she said. "What with the play and everything."

"Uh-huh." He clearly didn't believe her. "You know that some of the students involved in the dig go to school here, right?"

Francie hadn't known that. She sat up. "Who?" she couldn't resist asking.

"Mallory and Jackson." Francie could hear the smile in Nels's voice.

"Oh," Francie paused, trying to keep herself from asking any more questions, but before she could stop herself, "do you know them?" slipped out.

"Mallory is in one of my classes," Nels said, then added, "You know what her last name is?"

"No."

"Waxwing."

"As in *pipeline* Waxwing?"

"Uh-huh. That's her father."

"Blow me down."

"You want me to check it out?" Nels asked hopefully. "See what I can find out?"

Francie bit her lip. This might be a lead that could clear Theo. But, then again, who knows what might turn up if Nels started asking questions? Even more damning evidence against Theo was what. So she said, "Not really."

There was silence on the other end of the line.

"Look, Nels," Francie explained. "I'm in a brand-new school" (that was true) "trying to make friends" (that was a bald-faced lie), "have the lead in a play" (true), "and have a lot of homework" (not terribly true). "And I have to go."

There was a brief pause and then Nels cleared his throat. "Are you seeing someone else?" he asked.

"Seeing someone—? Absolutely not!" That, at least, was an absolutely true statement.

"So, we're still good?" Nels asked.

"Yeah, yeah, we're good," Francie said.

"Okay," Nels said, but Francie thought he sounded like he didn't believe her. But then, why should he? She supposed he could tell she was lying about something, and how could he know which things she said were true and which were not? Francie began to understand what Theo had been talking about when he said that keeping a secret could make a person into a liar. She had lied to every single person she'd talked to that night.

The person Francie found herself lying to the most was Raven. So much so that she wondered if Raven was on to her.

13

RAVEN IS ON TO FRANCIE

FRANCIE DID NOT DISCUSS the murder or her suspicions with anyone. Naturally, kids at school asked her who she thought did it, but she would act disinterested, after which they would immediately become disinterested in her.

Only in her little apartment, when she should have been studying, or during some classes when she was supposed to be working on something, did she try to puzzle it out. She drew maps showing all the cabins, noting where each person from the dig had been staying and a little sketch of the path through the woods that each would have taken to get back to the site. During study hall, she took a sheet of notebook paper and at the top wrote the presumed time of the murder, then under that heading wrote where everybody along the lake had been. Her list included the names of all of the suspects and their alibis, if she knew them, plus any other information she knew about them.

At the bottom of the list, she wrote simply, *Theo?* She stared at the name for a long time and then scribbled it out.

. . . . .

At the end of third-hour English, Ms. Broderick said, "Please pass your assignments to the back of the row."

Francie, who had been daydreaming, grabbed a paper from her notebook and passed it behind her to Raven. Raven was about to hand it to the person behind her when she stopped. She turned back to Francie, paper in hand, and whispered, "I don't think this is the paper you meant to hand in."

Francie snatched it back, mortified to see that it was her list of suspects. She stuffed the paper into her schoolbag and rifled through her notebook for the assignment, which she handed to Raven just as the bell was ringing.

Going through the lunch line, Raven took a quesadilla and began reciting, "*Mallory: showering at Mrs. Hansen's. Gretchen: swimming at Mrs. Hansen's. Jackson: grilling at Potter's. Pete: ditto. Potter vouched for both of them, so those two in the clear?*"

Francie's head swiveled. "Wait a minute," she said. "You remember all that from a two-second glance?"

"I have a good memory for details, when I want to remember."

"Geez," Francie said.

"And now you owe me," Raven said. "I saved you from something—intense embarrassment or possibly worse—but I can see you are not as disinterested in this murder as you pretend to be."

Francie didn't answer but nodded to the offered salad.

"You gotta admit the murder is more interesting than any box, silver or otherwise."

Francie shot Raven a warning glance; Raven pantomimed zipping her lips shut.

. . . . .

"All right, what all *do* you remember from that glance?" Francie said, after they were seated at their usual table, far from anyone's ears.

Raven folded her quesadilla into a small, fat square. "*Potter. Motive? Mrs. Hansen? Deaf, too old. Field trip students–slash–teacher,*" Raven recited. "*Long shot. Pipeline guy. Has motive.* A list of potential suspects of the murder, I presume," she added. "Everybody's wondering why you aren't sleuthing out this murder like you did the last time. What's going on? Why the secrecy?"

"The sheriff warned me away from it. She said she didn't want me messing with her investigation."

"Mmm," Raven said. "So, there was one more name on your list, wasn't there?"

"There was?" Francie mumbled, her mouth full of bread and cheese. "I don't remember any other."

"You crossed it out."

Francie shrugged.

"How come?" Raven said. Her dark eyes bored into Francie, and Francie wondered if Raven saw things in Francie's mind the way she seemed to see everything else.

"How come what?" Francie stalled.

"How come you crossed off that name?"

"I don't know," Francie mumbled. "Probably decided it wasn't important."

Raven slid herself and her tray to the far end of the table on the empty side of the cafeteria. Francie slid herself and her lunch along with her.

"Are you sure it's because you didn't want anyone else seeing that name?" Raven asked.

Francie was silent.

"It's Theo, isn't it?" Raven said softly. "You suspect Theo."

"No!" Francie protested. "I . . ." But nothing else came out of her mouth.

"You are a good actor but a terrible liar," Raven said. "Listen. It couldn't have been Theo."

"Absolutely couldn't have been," Francie agreed. She really had to scramble now to prevent this from getting out of hand.

"He's too good looking!" Raven laughed. Then, more seriously, "Plus, he's your brother. I mean, he wouldn't do that! Or wouldn't you at least *know* if he murdered someone?"

Francie swallowed the lump of bread that seemed stuck in her throat. She felt an itchy feeling in her head that meant she was going to cry. She cried more easily now that she wasn't sleeping very well, but she really didn't want to cry here in the cafeteria, in front of Raven or anyone else. But she felt her nose start to run. She grabbed her paper napkin and held it to her nose, then her eyes.

"You okay?" Raven said, her dark eyes a well of sympathy. Why had Francie ever thought Raven was ordinary looking? This girl had the kindest eyes on Earth. Those eyes—they saw everything! There was no hiding anything from her! Her name, which Francie had once thought was ironic, she now understood suited Raven perfectly.

"I don't know him very well, though," Francie choked out. "And to tell you the truth, I've been avoiding him since all this happened." Tears dripped down onto her lunch.

"Why don't you just ask him?" Raven said.

"I'm too afraid to know," Francie whispered. "I don't want to know. What if he did it?"

"All right, then," Raven said, glancing at the clock. "The only way to exonerate him is to figure out who did it and thereby prove it wasn't Theo."

"Or me," Francie said.

"What? Do you suspect yourself, too?"

"No, but the sheriff does."

"Really?" Raven said. "The plot thickens . . . and all the more reason to solve this sucker—and fast. You, me, and Jay."

"Jay?"

"He's the research king. We gotta have him."

14

TRIP TO ENCHANTMENT

THE LAKE WAS FLOODED with late-afternoon light. Sunlit lily pads made the surface of the water look as if it had been set with gold dishes. Francie and Raven stood on the shore at Sandy Beach Resort watching Jay and his golden retriever, Roy, play fetch.

"The thing is, Raven," Jay said, pausing to throw a tennis ball into the lake, then watching Roy plunge in after it, "if the oil isn't transported by pipeline, it's going to be transported by train, which is way more dangerous. More deadly accidents are likely to occur with train transport than with a pipeline."

"The thing is, Jay," Raven said, "it shouldn't be transported *at all*! We have to get off our dependence on fossil fuels. The biosphere can't handle it! And what about this?" Raven gestured out to the lake. "What happens to our water when there's an inevitable spill?"

Sandy came up behind them. "What's going on? Finally going to investigate that murder?"

Francie spun around. "No," she said. "Just arguing about fossil fuels."

"Oh," Sandy strolled out on the dock and the others followed. "Well, too bad you're not investigating," he said, as he lowered the boat from the launch, "because if you were, there's something I thought you might be interested in. But if you aren't . . ." He gestured for them to board.

"Tell us!" Raven chirped, stepping down into the boat.

Next Roy leapt in and, of course, immediately shook his wet coat, spraying water all over them.

Sandy started the motor, expertly pulled away from the dock, and swung the bow to face the far shore. "I don't know if it has anything to do with anything or not," he said, "but the customs and immigration people—the Canadian customs people, too— have been over here lately. Apparently they're investigating some kind of smuggling."

"No kidding!" Jay shouted over the motor. "Just like in Prohibition days."

"You know about that?" Sandy shouted back.

"Yeah, sure," Jay said.

Of course he does, Francie and Raven said wordlessly to each other.

"We're pretty close to Canada, and there was some rum running back in the '20s and '30s, during the Prohibition era," Jay hollered. "Shoot-outs and everything! But what are they smuggling now? Not liquor."

Sandy shook his head. "I don't know what it is. The customs people asked a bunch of questions but wouldn't tell us anything. It was all very hush-hush. I don't think they want anyone to know they're around, because they're trying to catch somebody."

As the boat pulled up to her aunts' dock, Francie wondered

aloud if it might have anything to do with the murder. Sandy shrugged and asked if they wanted a ride back—they did, maybe in a couple of hours. Everyone climbed out and he took off across the lake.

"Theo isn't here!" Astrid said when they stopped at the cabin.

"We haven't seen him for a couple of days," Jeannette added.

"Okay," Francie said. On the one hand, she was kind of relieved. She wouldn't have to explain to Theo what they were doing out there. On the other hand . . . where was he?

After promising to come back for hot cider and cookies, the three friends walked the leaf- and pine needle–strewn trail to the dig site. Roy bounded ahead of them.

"Are you worried about your brother?" Raven asked.

"I'm sure he's fine," Francie said, although she was not. She walked with her head down, absorbed in her thoughts.

"Hey," Raven said, "when we write the book about solving this mystery, what should the title be?"

"*The Perplexing Puzzle of the Perished Paleontologist*," Jay said.

Raven and Francie groaned.

"*The Theory of the Three Thoughtful Thespians*," he offered.

"No!" they shouted.

"*The Bewildering Breach of the Buried Bones*."

"Go away!" Francie said.

"Okay," Jay said, dropping behind them to snap pictures.

"Seriously, though," Raven said. "How about . . . hey! A clue in the trees!" she shouted.

"That is a totally lame title," Francie said.

"No! I mean there's *a clue in the trees!*" Raven pointed up at the branches overhead where something glinted in the sunlight.

"What *is* that?" Francie asked.

"Give me a boost," Raven said.

Francie cupped her hands and Raven put her foot in the offered step, boosting herself high enough to grab the item.

"It's just a hand spade," Raven said. "Like for gardening."

"What's it doing in a tree?" Francie wondered.

Raven stepped back down to earth and jammed the spade, sharp side down, into the dirt.

"Somebody must have just stuck it there and forgotten about it," Francie said, adding, "weird." She looked around and shivered a little bit. "Do you feel like maybe somebody else is out here?"

"Well, there's Jay," Raven said. Jay still lagged behind, taking pictures.

"I don't mean Jay." Francie shuddered and glanced into the woods. "I feel as if we're being watched."

"I guess Roy would sniff out a person, right?" Raven said, pointing at the dog, snuffling around the base of a tree.

The retriever could probably smell all the way to the great boreal forests of Canada, Francie thought. Imitating the dog, she breathed in the smell of fall: wet granite, damp bark, deep piles of old pine needles, the sour smell of fallen leaves.

"Okay," she said, glancing back to make sure Jay was out of earshot. Jay did not know of Francie's suspicions about her brother, and she wanted to keep it that way. "Tell me everything you remember about the day of the murder."

"There was a scarf," Raven said.

Francie flinched. Unconsciously she wound the wool scarf around her neck a little tighter.

"Yours?" Raven asked. "Except it was in Theo's hair."

"You noticed that?" Francie asked. There really was no point in trying to keep anything secret from Raven, she realized. Why had she even tried?

Raven nodded. "It must have fallen off on the path and he didn't notice it, I suppose. I picked it up."

"You!" Francie exclaimed. In her chest, it felt as if dry leaves spun and twirled, fluttered, leapt.

"I was thrilled," Raven said. "It was like when a damsel drops her handkerchief and a handsome prince picks it up, only in reverse."

"What?"

"*Hello.* It meant I had a reason to seek Theo out to return the scarf to him." Raven pantomimed the action, swooping down to pick up a fallen leaf and offering it to Francie.

"Did you find him?"

"I didn't see him," Raven said, "but I heard him. I heard him in the tent talking to Digby."

So, Francie thought, she wasn't the only one who knew Theo had spoken with Digby.

They arrived at the dig site to find yellow police tape still strung between trees, although looking a bit bedraggled. Roy paid no attention to it and ran right underneath it while the two girls stopped. Jay still lagged behind.

"Is this still off-limits?" Raven asked.

"They probably just forgot to take down the tape," Francie said. She lifted it and Raven crawled under. "So what did you do with the scarf?"

"Since I could hardly barge into the tent and say, 'Sir, you've dropped your beautiful floral scarf,'" Raven said as she held the tape up for Francie, "I just left it outside where he would see it when he left. Right there." She gestured to a spruce tree's low-hanging boughs.

"The sheriff says it was the murder weapon," Francie admitted. "The scarf, I mean. Digby was strangled with it, apparently."

"Creepy," Raven said. "Is that why the sheriff suspects you?"

"I suppose," Francie said.

"Well, the scarf would have been accessible to anyone and everyone," Raven said, echoing Francie's thoughts. At least, thought Francie, it made Theo less of a suspect. Or *did* it?

As if reading her thoughts, Raven said, "Why do you suspect Theo? Where was he and what was he doing during the time of the murder?"

Francie didn't know. Why, oh why, had she fallen asleep then, of all times?

"After I found Digby, when he was . . . um, dead," Francie said, "I went through the woods—I was confused and took the wrong path, and when I came out of the woods, I saw Theo washing his hands in the lake. It just looked so suspicious."

"Okay, smarty-pants," Raven said, "why would he need to wash his hands if he'd just *strangled* someone?"

"Oh," Francie said. "Yeah. Why? I don't know. It just seems like you'd wash your hands if you killed somebody."

"Have you ever asked him?"

"No," Francie said. "I kept waiting for him to explain himself. Why did he argue with Digby? Why was he gone at the same time Digby was murdered? Why was he washing his hands in the lake? I wanted him to tell me, but I didn't want to have to ask him."

"Well, I think you should ask."

"What if he lies?"

"Why do you think he'll lie?"

How could she answer without telling Raven everything—everything she'd been taught never to talk about to anyone?

"Where's Roy?" Jay asked, coming up behind them.

Raven looked around. "He was . . . I don't know!"

"Should we be worried?" Francie asked.

"Roy!" Jay called and crashed off into the brush.

Raven and Francie shouted Roy's name a few times, then Raven said, "He'll turn up. He's a dog, right?"

"I suppose," Francie agreed.

"So, back to the suspects!" Raven said cheerily. "There was a cook here, right?"

"She was done for the year," Francie said.

Raven squinted off in the distance so intently that Francie turned around to look behind her. "What?" Francie's heart raced. "Do you see Roy?"

"Are you sure the cook wasn't here?" Raven asked.

"What? Why?"

"When we were here that day, the flap on the cook tent was open. I know it was the cook tent because I remember seeing pots and pans and utensils hanging from a kind of pegboard. But when we came by again, there was something missing."

Francie stared at Raven. "Whoa. You really remember that?"

"I just remember things like that. Details. I don't know why," Raven said.

"What was missing?"

"Each item on the pegboard had an outline. I suppose so the item would go back where it belonged. When we passed by the tent the second time, the big knife was no longer there. But you could see its outline."

Francie stared at Raven for a long time. "Wow," she said, shaking her head. "Wow."

"Roy!" Raven cried. "There you are!"

They could just see the top of the dog's head some distance away.

"What's the deal? Is he in a hole or something?" Francie said. Then, with some wiggling, the rest of the very filthy dog appeared and, tongue hanging out, bounded over to them.

"Jay! Your dog is here!" Raven yelled.

Roy shook, flinging damp dirt from his fur while Jay staggered out of the woods, covered with stickers and burrs. "Where you been, boy?" he cooed, kneeling and throwing his arms around the dog. "He never does that! Well, not very often anyway," Jay said to the girls. Then, yanking his hand away, said, "Ick! He's sticky!"

"He was in a hole or something," Raven said, walking to where the dog had appeared. "Hey!" she shouted back to the others, "this is no ordinary hole."

Jay and Francie had started toward Raven when they were stopped by a voice behind them, saying, "Just what do you think you're doing?"

15
THEO IS GONE

SHERIFF WARNER stood with hands on hips. "What are you kids doing here?" she said.

What is *she* doing here? Francie wondered.

"This is still off-limits," the sheriff continued. "Didn't you notice the tape? Come on out of there."

The threesome climbed back under the yellow tape and started toward the cabin, the dog bounding on ahead.

"I'll talk to you later!" the sheriff called after them.

"Something to look forward to," Raven muttered.

Seated in the cabin living room, with the sky growing dark outside, the aunts plied the three sleuths with cocoa and cookies—and questions.

"Well, Frenchy," Astrid leaned toward her, her eyes bright with interest, "what have you learned?"

"Learned? You mean at school?"

"For the love of Mike!" Astrid said. "No! What have you learned about the murder?"

Obviously, Francie's aunts weren't buying the ruse that she wasn't interested. She gnawed at the edge of a cookie. *Murder weapon—cookie?* popped into her head. "Well, one thing Raven noticed was that a butcher knife went missing from the cook tent."

"Ooh, a butcher knife!" Astrid exclaimed. "How thrilling! But it wasn't the murder weapon. The victim was strangled, not stabbed."

Francie swallowed and wondered how her aunts knew that, but she went on. "We also know that anybody could have picked up the presumed murder weapon, aka the scarf."

"So, who took the knife and why?" Raven asked. "And where did it go?"

Francie reached down and pretended to pet Roy, who was lying at her feet. He readily accepted the offered cookie. When her hand brushed his still sticky fur, she wondered again where he'd gone and what he'd gotten into. He smelled strange. Not doggish or gross, just . . . strange.

"That knife is a puzzler," Jeannette agreed. "So far as we know, it didn't turn up at the dig site or in the investigative report."

"You've seen the report?" Francie was a little incredulous.

"Well, not officially," Jeannette said, glancing at Astrid. "But we had the opportunity to glance at it."

Francie had to remember not to underestimate her aunts. They had broken out of jail the previous summer and seemed to have talents most people would not expect. Adding to the mystery of her already strange family, Francie thought.

"Who do you think could have done it?" Astrid asked, passing the cookie plate once again. Only Jay was brave enough to take another.

"My dad's a dentist," he explained in response to Francie's and Raven's raised eyebrows, then mumbled, his mouth still full of cookie. "Maybe it was one of the interns."

"Oh, they were all such nice young people," Astrid said. "Do you really think any of them would actually kill someone?" She seemed to relish the word *kill*, Francie thought, something that would have been alarming if Aunt Astrid weren't so cute!

"Mallory?" Francie said. "Or Mallory's dad? The pipeline guy."

"He was actually kind of nice, though," Raven said. "He probably did save our lives when we fell in that trench."

"And he didn't press charges," Francie added. She pictured the man worriedly clutching his hard hat at the ER. Didn't seem like the murderous type at all.

"Well, what about—" Francie stopped in midsentence as the door opened.

Five heads swiveled to regard the sheriff who stepped in, followed by two deputies.

Sheriff Warner's eyes drifted over the others and settled on Francie.

"Care for a cookie?" Francie held the plate out to the sheriff, desperately hoping she would take one.

She declined.

"Sure?" Francie said. "They're very . . . substantial."

The sheriff ignored her. "We were hoping to find your brother," she said. "Is he around?"

"No," Francie said. Her aunts shook their heads.

"Any idea where he might be? We are trying to locate his whereabouts."

"Why?" Francie said.

Ignoring Francie's question, the sheriff asked, "Do you know how we can reach him?"

"No," Francie said, and repeated, "why?"

"If you hear from him, let my office know, all right?" Sheriff Warner handed her a card and pointed to the phone number.

As soon as the sheriff and the deputies left, the aunts looked at Francie. Astrid rose, toddled over to Francie, put her hands on her shoulders, and said, "This does not look good. That report we mentioned earlier? It suggests that Theo is the prime suspect. I think the sheriff plans to arrest him. It's up to you, Francie—you have to prove he didn't do it!"

16
DRAGON BONE

IN THE LUNCH LINE the next day, Francie pushed her tray along absentmindedly, thinking about Theo. No one had heard from him for days. Where had he gone? Had he just disappeared like he did sometimes? Had he run away because he knew he was a suspected murderer? Or because he *was* a murderer? Or had something terrible happened to him? And how could she find out?

A gravelly sounding voice interrupted her thoughts. "Beans?" the voice said.

Francie looked up to see the lunch lady standing behind a steaming pan, wearing a hairnet and a scowl. But this time, Francie realized how it was she knew her: that lunch lady had been the cook at the dig site that summer.

Francie couldn't help it; she flinched, whether it was from surprise or the scowl, she didn't know.

The woman narrowed her eyes and aimed her green-eyed stare at Francie. "Beans?" she growled again.

Francie looked at the grayish-green beans, shook her head, and said, "No, thank you." She quickly pushed her tray as far away from the woman as she could go, foregoing the mac and cheese, then picked up a dish of apple crisp, only to have it suddenly yanked away from her. The formidable-looking lunch lady clung to one edge of Francie's dish of apple crisp.

"Didn't your mother ever tell you that if you don't eat your vegetables you can't have dessert?" the woman growled.

"You call that a lunch?" Raven asked when Francie sat down across from her with nothing but a carton of milk on her tray.

"Raven!" Francie gasped. "That lunch lady gave me a really nasty look just now when I didn't want the beans. It was like she was giving me the evil eye. Then she wouldn't let me have the apple crisp!"

"Oh, Evil Iris?" Jay said, sliding in next to Francie.

"That's what everybody calls her," Raven added.

"She does that to everyone," Jay put in. "It's like she doesn't want you to eat or something." He plopped some of his mac and cheese on Francie's tray. "If you want it," he said.

"Thanks." Francie poked at it. "I guess. But, you guys! I remember something. The lunch lady—Iris—was the cook at the dig site."

"No way!" Jay and Raven said together, both looking over their shoulders at the lunch line.

Their heads snapped back around in unison. "She's staring at us!" Raven said.

"Well?" Francie said. "*You* were staring at *her!*"

"Think she could be the killer?" Jay stabbed at his mac and cheese with his spoon as if he were trying to kill it. "She's definitely trying to kill us off with this food."

"Maybe you should start bringing lunch from home," Raven said, "like I said."

"She couldn't have been the killer, though," Francie mused. "She wasn't working there anymore. And nobody saw her there, either."

"Maybe she was there and nobody noticed her," Jay suggested.

They all turned to look at Iris, whose wide body was just then darkening the door to the kitchen. She clomped over to the plastic garbage can and loudly scraped something from a dish into the bin. They could hear the sticky *shlikk-shlikk* of her shoes from where they were sitting.

"Nope," they said in unison, then turned back to their lunches.

Francie's thoughts wandered back to Theo and where he might be. When she tuned back in, Jay was saying, ". . . a lot of illegal poaching of rhinos and tigers. It's an especially big problem because, like, the bones are used in medicines sometimes, especially in Asia. Killing rhinos just for their horns. It's seriously really sad."

"Yeah," Raven said. "I've seen some gruesome pictures of dead rhinos with just their horns cut off. It's disgusting."

"There's a long tradition of using bones and other weird stuff in medicine." Jay pulled out a bunch of papers from his backpack. "In the official Pharmacopoeia of the College of Physicians of London of 1678 and 1724 they list as medicines—" Jay found what he was looking for and read, "Unicorn's horn, human fat and skulls, dog's dung, toads, vipers, and worms."

"Gawd," Raven said. "That is gross. But—"

"I'm getting to it," Jay said. "It turns out that in China, they're still using bone. Tiger bone and rhino horn as previously mentioned. But also something called Long Gu."

"What's that?"

"Dragon bone."

"Dragon bone," Francie repeated.

"Yeah, but it's not really dragon bones."

"*Really?*" Raven said sarcastically.

"*Obviously*, it's not dragon bone," Jay said. "But guess what it is."

"Unicorn horn," said Raven.

"Griffin femurs," Francie offered.

"No. It is actually mammoth and mastodon bones. See, when the people of ancient times found these huge and strange bones, they tried to imagine what kind of giant creatures there were that had roamed the earth. Maybe dragons, right? How else do you explain them? But now, even though they know they are mammoth or mastodon bones, they are still prized as a treatment for . . . ," Jay read from a printout, "insomnia, palpitation, irritability, mania, or neurotic disorders. Dragon bone powder is regularly prescribed as a sedative."

"You know what?" Raven said. "That is very interesting because Dakotas collected pieces of mastodon bones for their medicine bags. That was here, in Minnesota."

"So maybe that's what's being smuggled," Jay said. "The mastodon bones."

"That's just what I said!" Raven said. "Right, Frenchy? Frenchy?"

Francie stared back at them, speechless.

"Frenchy?" Raven and Jay said together.

"After school," Francie said, "meet me at Muskie Bait."

17

HALLOWEEN

"YOU REALIZE WE HAVE A PARTY to get ready for, right?" Jay said, as the three friends walked past cobweb-festooned shrubs and trees hung with little plastic ghosts. Jack-o'-lanterns leered at them from front porches. "Costumes? Makeup?"

"I know, I know," Francie said. "This shouldn't take long. You'll still have time to get to the party."

"Dance," Raven put in.

"Whatever it is."

"What do you mean, 'You'll still have time'?" Jay squawked. "Aren't you going?"

"Sure," Francie said, unconvincingly.

"What's your costume?"

"Costume? I have to have a costume?"

"Uh, hello?" Jay said. "It's Halloween!"

"Are you going?" Francie asked Raven.

Raven shook her head.

"If you're not, then I'm not," Francie said.

"You gu-uys!" Jay said. "You have to!"

The giant muskie that served as the entrance to the closed-for-the-season Muskie Bait shop loomed. The peeling green and white exterior gave the impression of a half-scaled fish. Its faded pink gums and once white but now yellow-brown teeth were so convincingly decayed you could practically smell bad fish breath.

"So," Raven said. "What are we doing here?"

Francie sighed. "The first day of school, if you remember, everybody thought Muskie Bait was vandalized. It wasn't."

"And you would know this because . . . ?" Jay said.

"You cannot—*cannot*—tell anyone this. Not anyone," Francie said.

"Sworn to secrecy," Raven and Jay crossed their hearts and did an impromptu secret handshake.

"That night, I was with Theo. Here. We were chased into this place."

"Chased!"

"By I don't know who—some wing nut in a trench coat. I don't know why, either."

"Was this guy chasing you or Theo?"

"Why would anyone be chasing me? I've been thinking about it, and I think Theo had something with him, something he may have hidden inside here somewhere," she said. "He gave me his backpack," Francie handed Raven her schoolbag, "and he groped around along the muskie's teeth for a while . . ." Francie ran her hands along the teeth, not knowing what she expected to find. "With everything that was going on, I didn't really stop to wonder why he was doing that. And it was dark, so I couldn't see much."

"What does your brother do, Francie?" Raven asked.

"Do?" Francie said.

"Like, for work?" Raven said. "Is he a student, or what?"

"I don't know," Francie said. "He travels a lot. Something with archaeology."

"He's an archaeologist?"

"Sort of? Not really? I guess I don't really know."

"Did he come back because of the dig?"

Francie paused midtooth and turned to Raven. Had he? She had been trying to force herself not to think of his argument with Digby. Now she forced herself to think of it. How did he know Digby? And why had they argued?

Francie took Raven by the shoulders, staring at her. "Something's going on. Something we have no idea about."

"Obviously," Raven said.

"No, Raven. I mean something big. Bigger than mastodon bones—it has to be." A familiar fear—the fear that Theo was in trouble—seized her again. "Theo is tangled up in it somehow. Oh, if only I knew what was going on!" she cried.

"He's your brother, by the way," Raven said. "Why don't you just ask him?"

"He won't tell me. He's a master of not telling me things." Francie went back to feeling along the muskie's dirty brown teeth, wiggling each one along the line. "This fish is in need of some dental work," she said. "Oh, I know it's here somewhere, I know it." And then, "Ah ha!" she said, holding up a lump of something, about as big as her hand, but heavier, bulkier—in fact, about the size and shape of one of the muskie's teeth.

"Did you just pull one of the teeth out?" Raven asked.

"Oh crap. I did." Francie tried to fit it back where it had been. But it just didn't fit. "It seems like it was just stuck there," she said.

"Let me see that," Jay said, and Francie handed him the lump. They all moved under the streetlight outside. Jay turned it this way and that, then whispered, "I think this might be an actual tooth. Of a very large animal."

"But why would your brother put it there?" Raven said.

"To hide it? Maybe the guy who was chasing us was after it? I mean, that seems like the most sense, doesn't it?"

"We need to find out what kind of tooth this is," Jay said. "Let's ask my dad."

"Your dad?" Raven asked.

"He's a dentist," Jay explained.

Raven handed Francie her schoolbag, and Francie stuffed the thing into it, hefted it over her shoulder, and the three of them stepped out into the damp wind.

"I'll wait outside," Raven said when they approached Jay's house.

"What? No!" Jay said. "It's cold out here."

"I'm okay," Raven said.

Francie looked at her with concern. Why would she want to wait out in the cold when she could go in the warm house? Jay decided for her when he opened the door and pulled her inside.

They were greeted by Jay's dad, who said, "Come on in. It's colder than a polar bear's toenails out there." He looked at all of them over his reading glasses. Francie couldn't help but notice that his eyes rested a little longer on Raven. Living in a town like Walpurgis, he'd have to be used to seeing Native people, Francie thought, just maybe not in his own house.

"Another cold wave from Canada," Jay said.

His dad recovered from the surprise—or whatever it was—in time to deliver the punch line, "You'd think they'd weatherstrip the border!"

Jay shrugged apologetically, dug the whatever-it-was out of

the schoolbag, and handed it to his father. "Dad, do you know if this is a tooth and, if so, what kind of animal it's from?"

Before his dad even pushed his glasses up onto his nose into reading mode, Jay was Googling pictures of dinosaur teeth and comparing them to the pointed lump in his dad's hands. "Doesn't it look like this *Tarbosaurus bataar* tooth?" he asked. "Only I bet it's even bigger than that." He stared intently at his phone for a moment, then dashed away down the hall, tripped over a throw rug, recovered, and disappeared into another room.

"This dinosaur did not use good dental hygiene," Dr. Rawlings said. "But do you know what dinosaur had the healthiest teeth and gums?"

"No idea," Francie said.

"The flossoraptor!" Dr. Rawlings mimed hitting a drumset cymbal.

Francie and Raven emitted dutiful chuckles. Jay, returning with a tape measure in hand, set to work measuring the tooth.

"You guys!" Jay nearly breathed the words.

"What?" Francie and Raven breathed back at him.

"This tooth is bigger than the biggest dinosaur tooth ever found. If it is a dinosaur tooth—a real one, that is—then it probably came from—"

"The biggest dinosaur ever!" Raven and Francie said simultaneously, then, also simultaneously, slugged each other.

"You kids!" Dr. Rawlings said. "I thought it was Halloween, not April Fools'!" He tucked his glasses into his shirt pocket and ambled away, shaking his head.

Francie and Raven stepped back outside, the tooth tucked into Francie's schoolbag. They agreed to stash the fossil at Francie's apartment, but they hadn't gone two blocks when Francie got that weird feeling that they were being followed.

It wasn't just a feeling. A truck drove up just behind them, moving slowly along as they walked.

"Are those guys trying to intimidate us, or what?" Francie asked Raven.

"Are you intimidated?"

"No."

"Me neither." Raven looked over at the truck, where the two boys smirked at her. "Did you want something?" she called over to the boys.

"Just making sure you don't trespass on somebody's property," the boy in the passenger seat said out his open window.

"We're on the city sidewalk," Francie said. "Public property."

"Well, stay there," shouted the driver, then sped up, did a U-turn, and peeled away.

"What was that about?" Francie said. "Was it about the protest? Did you know we were trespassing that day?"

"I thought it was tribal land," Raven said.

"That's not what the sheriff says."

"Is the law always right, Miss Antigone? Sometimes you have to defy the law to do what's right—right?"

"So you knew we were trespassing—or whatever?"

"No," Raven said. "Actually, I didn't."

Francie glanced over her shoulder. The truck was disappearing around a corner, but she noticed something more disturbing. "Who wears a trench coat and fedora in Walpurgis?" she said.

"What?" Raven said. "Nobody."

"Somebody does." Francie quickly steered the two of them toward the center of town. "And whoever it is . . . is following us."

Downtown businesses were hosting Halloween-themed events. Candy was involved, so swarms of small children mobbed the streets, their costumes buried under parkas, hats, and mittens. Shimmery blue gowns hung below plaid jackets, boldly striped pirate pants poked out from under coats, masks perched on the stocking hats of goblins and ghosts and princesses and fairies.

Francie glanced over her shoulder. Trench Coat was closing the gap.

"Hurry!" Francie yelped, and she and Raven tore down the sidewalk, rounded the corner, and for a moment were out of sight of Trench Coat. Francie took the opportunity to lift the tooth from her schoolbag and drop it into the pillowcase of an inattentive Ninja Turtle. Entranced by a magic show in front of the hardware store, the tot dragged his trick-or-treat bag along behind him, seemingly unaware of his new prize.

Francie pulled Raven into the drugstore. From there she could watch the Ninja Turtle out the window.

"What's going on?" Raven whispered.

"It's okay," Francie stared out the window, determined to not let the tot out of her sight. "I got rid of it; it's in that Ninja Turtle's pillowcase."

"What?" Raven whispered. "You put that tooth in a kid's trick-or-treat bag? Are you kidding me?"

"It kept Trench Coat from getting it, didn't it?" she whispered back.

"Do you girls need any help?" A store employee approached, stood a few feet away, crossed her arms, and glared at them.

"No, thanks," Francie said.

"Can I help you find anything?" the clerk asked again, staring at Raven.

"We're fine." Francie tried to return the clerk's stare, but the woman's gaze was fixed on Raven.

Raven executed an almost imperceptible eye roll.

Geez, Francie thought. Did Raven deal with this kind of crap all the time?

"She just has to *call her brother*," Raven said and poked Francie. "Then we'll skedaddle."

The store clerk stood her ground. Francie glanced out the window. Fortunately, the young trick-or-treater moved about as fast as a regular, non–Ninja-type turtle, so Francie looked down just as long as it took to find Theo's number. When she looked up again, somebody had the little boy by the hand and was pulling him and his pillowcase along at a pretty good clip. Somebody in a trench coat and fedora.

Francie grabbed Raven by the arm and bolted for the door.

The crowd on Main Street had grown. Fortunately, the crowd consisted of mostly kids eight years old or younger, which made them easy to see over. It also made them easy to stumble over. When she got clear, Francie made a dash for it and, rushing up behind the two figures, impulsively grabbed the pillowcase away from the child.

The trench coat turned, and Francie came face-to-face with . . .

"Phoebe?" Francie said.

Raven threw her hands to her face in embarrassment.

"What is your guys' problem?" Phoebe said. "I don't believe it—stealing kids' trick-or-treat bags? Jeez!" She grabbed the bag back. Or tried to, but Francie had a firm grip on it. A tug-of-war of sorts ensued.

"I . . . uh . . . ," Francie stammered. "Um . . . why are you wearing a trench coat?"

"Duh! Halloween?" Phoebe said.

"Ri . . . ight," Francie said.

Phoebe ripped the bag out of Francie's hands. "I hope you realize you're traumatizing my little brother," she huffed, then hurried down the street, yanking the little turtle along behind her.

18
THE LIE DETECTOR

FRANCIE AND RAVEN pressed their faces up against the glass doors of the school, which were locked.

"There he is," Raven said, rattling the door. Mr. Redburn was busy setting up a table in the lobby outside the gymnasium where the dance was to be held. "He'll have Phoebe's number, even though you don't."

"What about you? Why don't you have it?"

"Why would I have Phoebe's number?" Raven said. "I don't even have a phone!"

In response to their pounding, Mr. Redburn looked up, walked over, opened the door, and said, "Dance doesn't start until eight o'clock."

"We know, but we need a phone number from you."

"Whose?"

"Phoebe's," Raven said.

"Why?" Mr. Redburn sounded skeptical.

Reading his face, Francie could see he knew that although she and Phoebe played sisters in the play, they were not friends. Not that it was a secret or anything.

"Long story," Raven said. "But it's kind of urgent."

"You'll see her in a few hours," he said. "Can't it wait until then?"

"Urgent!" Raven repeated.

Redburn sighed and opened the door, and the girls stepped inside. He retrieved his phone and gave them Phoebe's number, and then Raven said, "Hey, would it be okay if we borrowed some costumes? You know, for the party? I mean, can we borrow something from the costume shop?"

"I don't need a costume!" Francie protested.

But Mr. Redburn was already sliding the key to the costume room off his ring.

"Okay," he said, handing it to Raven. "But nothing from the show!" he hollered as they hurried down the hall.

As soon as they were out of earshot, Raven said, "Okay, little Missy, make the call."

Francie punched in the number and waited until Phoebe picked up.

"What do you want?" Phoebe asked.

A line from the play popped into Francie's head: *Go away, Ismene. I shall be hating you soon.* She said instead, "I don't know if your brother has found any weird thing in his trick-or-treat bag, but it's mine."

"What *was* that thing? Gross!" Phoebe said.

"What *was*?" Francie repeated, her skin prickling.

Raven's eyes widened.

"Eww!" Phoebe said. "Why did you put that in my brother's bag, anyway? Was that some kind of joke? You're sick!"

Francie tried to keep her voice level. "Where is it now?" she asked.

There was a long silence at the end of the line. "I don't have to tell you."

"Phoebe!" Francie cried. "Look, I know you don't like me. I'm sorry I got the part of Antigone. I told Mr. Redburn to give the part to you—"

"You did?" Phoebe cut in.

"Yes," Francie said. "At auditions."

There was silence on the other end while Phoebe considered that.

"So can I get it back?" Francie said, finally.

After another long pause, Phoebe said, "Fine. I'll bring it tonight." She hung up.

Francie turned to Raven. "She says she'll bring it tonight."

"Well, then!" Raven said, cheerily. "We better get costumes!"

"Do we really need . . . ," Francie protested, as Raven took her arm and steered her down the hall, deeper into the school, ". . . costumes?"

"Yes, we do," Raven said.

"Why?"

"Because," Raven inserted the key in the door and led Francie into the room. "Remember what we were talking about before? About *The Case of the Unfortunately Flawed Field Trip?*"

"Um . . . no?" Francie said.

"I'm just saying, maybe we can find out something."

"O . . . kay?" Francie looked around the room at the racks of costumes, the makeup table. "In here?"

"Not *exactly* here," Raven said. "But it turns out that behind all those costumes is a closet, and through the closet is another door, a door that leads to Redburn's office! And if we're lucky, this key opens that door, too. Come on!"

They batted their way through old prom dresses and wedding gowns to a closet, opened the closet door to face more hanging clothes, fur coats, and shelves full of school and theater supplies—paint, stage lighting, and cardboard boxes full of who knows what.

"See? It's just like Narnia! You know, through the wardrobe?"

Just as Raven was about to put the key in the door to Redburn's office, they heard the door to the costume shop rattling. Retreating from the closet, and pulling Francie along with her, Raven grabbed a bolt of blue fabric, wrapped pretty much all of it around Francie, and immediately started jabbing pins into it.

"Boo!" Jay leapt into the room dressed in all black, painted in glow-in-the-dark paint to look like a skeleton.

"Geez, Jay," Raven said, pressing her hand to her heart.

"Pretty scary costume, huh?" he said. "How did you know it was me? Oh, shoot, I forgot the mask." He slid a fabric mask over his head, turning his face into a skull with gaping eyes. "Now do you know who it is?"

"By the way, Jay," Raven said, "right now this is the *girls'* dressing room."

"All skeletons are created equal. Hey, you know why skeletons are so calm?"

"No, why?" Francie said.

"Because nothing gets under their skin."

Francie laughed and Raven said, "Jay, you spend too much time with your dad."

"Why do you say that?"

"Never mind," Raven said.

"Ow!" Francie yelped. "Watch it with the pins. But, Jay, what are you doing here, anyway?"

"I found out something." Jay glanced over his shoulder, then shut the door. "About Redburn," he whispered.

"Weawy?" Raven asked through the straight pins in her teeth.

"Yeah," Jay said. "After you guys left, I did a little digging and found out that he and Digby were classmates in graduate school. You know—paleontology?"

"Ee oh ad," Raven said, talking around the pins.

"'We know that,'" Francie translated.

"Yeah, but I don't think they were friends, like Redburn says."

"No?" Francie said. "Ouch! Geez, Raven! You're going to draw blood!"

"It was Redburn who was the rising star in grad school," Jay continued. "He was all set to become the next Louis Leakey or somebody."

"Louis Leakey?"

"The guy who discovered *Homo erectus*."

"What?" Raven and Francie giggled.

"Seriously," Jay said. "An extinct species of the human lineage, having upright stature and a well-evolved postcranial skeleton, but with a smallish brain, low forehead, and protruding face."

"Okay, the giggling is immature," Raven said, giggling.

"So, what happened?" Francie asked.

"Redburn dropped out of school."

"Why?"

"I don't know, but the interesting thing is, it seems that Digby stepped into the limelight about then."

"If he was such a hotshot, why was he here, digging up mastodon bones? I don't think mastodon bones are that big of a deal."

"Exactly," Jay said. "For a guy who's been head of major expeditions all over the world, you'd think he'd have better things to do."

"Maybe he was looking for something bigger than mastodon bones," Raven said.

"Like . . . what?"

"Isn't there some kind of legend about a treasure out at Enchantment?" Raven stood back and admired her handiwork.

Francie had so many pins sticking in her she felt like a porcupine. Not daring to move an inch, she said stiffly, "Wait. What? Does everybody know that story? I thought it was just an Enchantment Lake tale that grown-ups told their kids to keep them busy. Like, 'Kid, go outside and look for buried treasure.' That kind of thing."

"Around here? Everybody's heard about it," Jay said. "Not sure everybody believes it."

"What do they say the treasure is?" Francie asked.

"What *don't* they say the treasure is?" Jay said. "Bootlegged whiskey ... copper ... gold—"

"Gold?"

"Oh, yeah, there was a gold rush around here in the late 1800s."

"Did they find anything?"

"Nothing worth the money it took to get it out of the ground. But now they're starting to rethink that," Jay said. "There are even stories that there are works of art stashed out there, or ancient artifacts, or whatever. But that's pretty out there, as theories go."

There were three sharp raps on the door, then Redburn's voice: "You guys in there?"

Jay, Raven, and Francie looked at each other, then Francie called out, "We're in here, Mr. Redburn. Come on in." Then, before Redburn stepped in, she whispered to her friends, "Might as well find out what he knows."

Raven mumbled something about looking for a costume and disappeared among the racks of clothes. Jay stared intently at his phone. Francie could see it would be up to her to try to find out what she could from their director.

"We were just wondering about your college days, or was it your *post*-college days when you knew Digby?" Francie asked.

Redburn looked at Francie, since she was the only one looking back.

"Graduate school," he said.

"Oh, right," she said. "So I guess you were friends then?"

"Yes, that's right," Redburn said. "Listen. Are you about finished? I've got to lock up. You're going to have to clear out."

"But wait. Raven doesn't have a costume yet."

"Fine," he growled. "Make it snappy," he called into the clothes racks.

"Can I ask you another question?" Francie asked. "About those graduate school days?"

"What?" Redburn shot back sharply. He started shoving all the bottles and tubes and containers of stage makeup against the long mirror that ran the length of the counter.

"Why didn't you complete your doctorate?" she asked.

His head snapped up. "I don't see why—" he began, then started over, saying simply, "Fell down a flight of stairs and got pretty banged up. Broke a bunch of bones, had a head injury, there was a lot of rehab. Found it hard to concentrate."

"I don't mean to get too personal, but is that how you got your limp?" Francie asked.

Jay glanced at her, unable to keep his eyebrows level—they nearly disappeared under his hairline.

"Might I ask why you're asking all these questions?" Redburn said.

"I'm just curious," Francie said. "So, like, what would your graduate degree have been in? And what happened to your dissertation—all your research and stuff?"

Redburn's nostrils flared. He glanced in the mirror and smoothed his hair before saying, "Listen. That's it for questions and for the use of this room. I gotta go and I gotta lock this up."

"I'll wait for you guys outside," Jay said, heading out.

Raven returned in a long hooded cape, the hood pulled so far over her head it was hard to tell who was under there.

The three of them walked the quiet school corridors at first without talking. Other than the sound of their footfalls, the *shoosh* of Raven's cape, and the rustling bolt of fabric in which Francie was swathed, it was quiet.

Finally, Jay whispered, "Redburn was lying."

"How do you know that?" Raven whispered back.

All of them scanned the hallway behind them, in front, and down an intersecting corridor. No sign of Redburn.

"He exhibited all the signs," Jay went on. "He didn't use the words *I* or *me* if he could help it. He fidgeted. He busied himself straightening things that didn't need straightening. Didn't look anybody in the eyes."

"How do you know those are signs of lying?" Francie asked.

"What do you think I was doing on my phone? I was Googling it as you were grilling him. And *boom*! He went right down the list: four out of ten surefire signs of lying."

"The real question is," Raven said, "if he was lying, why? What was he lying about? How do we find out the truth? We know he was classmates with Digby. We know he fell down a flight of stairs. We know he was a rising star. So, if he was lying, what was he lying about?"

"Here's something strange . . . ," Francie said, slowly. "Back at auditions, he warned me from investigating the murder. He said I needed to put my time and energy into the play. He said something about me being a role model, blah blah blah. Do you think he might have given me the big part just to keep me busy—to distract me from the investigation?"

"And that weird field trip," Jay added, "which now seems

like maybe it was all a cover story. It got him out there on some pseudo-legit business and gave him a kind of alibi, except the thing was, when would he have killed Digby? He was with us at the site, on the pontoon—he was with us the whole time."

"Only he wasn't," Raven said. "Not the whole time." She stopped and stared into the distance as if she could see all the way to Enchantment Lake.

The other two stopped and stared, too, as if they might see whatever she was seeing.

"Wait, wait, wait!" Raven said in a hoarse whisper. "Phoebe was the last one back! We had to wait for her. In fact, Mr. Redburn had to go back and look for her! I'd almost forgotten."

"Could it be Phoebe?" Jay said.

They paused to consider, then all said at once, "Naw."

"It's gotta be *him!*" Jay said, wide-eyed. "Our own director! That is super-creepy. What are we going to do?"

"We have to report him to the sheriff!" Raven said.

"No," Francie said firmly.

"Why not?" Raven asked.

"The sheriff and Redburn are on a first-name basis," Francie told them. "I think they might be a thing. Dating? Maybe. Sheriff Warner slipped up when she was talking to me and called him by his first name. Maybe that doesn't mean anything, or maybe it means they're chums. I just got the feeling there's something going on between them."

"Oh, boy," Jay said.

"So I think we have to get more evidence—something more substantial—before we go to anybody with an accusation."

"So we have to keep going to rehearsal as if everything is just fine?" Raven asked.

"And what about right now?" Jay said. "Because, besides Redburn, we are the only ones in this school."

"OMG," Raven whispered. "We are all alone in this school with a murderer!"

"Well, let's get out of here," Jay squawked.

"We can't," Francie said. "Or at least I can't. I left my phone back in the costume shop. I'll just run back and get it. You guys can go if you want."

"We'll wait here," Raven said. "Hurry!"

Francie moved somewhat like a homecoming float, she supposed, down the long hall. As soon as she rounded the corner, out of sight of her friends, the sound of her boot heels echoing in the empty hallway made her slow her steps. It was suddenly so dark. And quiet. Except, that is, for the noises she supposed were there all the time but never noticed during the school day: the tick of a wall clock, the ping of a pipe, the strange creakings and groanings of an old building—tiny sounds suddenly leapt out at her as slightly sinister.

She hadn't left her phone; it was secure in the pocket of her jeans, now buried under yards of blue fabric. But she had realized during her conversation with Raven and Jay that she still clutched the key to the costume shop—the key that Raven said led into Redburn's office. It was too good an opportunity to pass up. What if she could find something that incriminated Redburn? Or at least let Theo off the hook? She had decided to go by herself because she didn't want to get her friends in trouble. At least that's what she told herself. But maybe it was because if she found anything incriminating about Theo, she wanted to be able to keep that information to herself.

Using the key that Raven had given her, Francie unlocked the door to the costume shop, closed it behind her, then pushed her way through the old prom dresses to reach the closet.

She found the door Raven had said led to Redburn's office and slipped the key into the lock. It fit; it turned; the door opened, just as Raven said it would, and then she was inside the office—a jumble of boxes and piles of books and papers and . . . bones! Bones all over the place! Some kind of animal skull used as a bookend, the entire skeleton of something, and individual bones gathering dust on shelves.

Creepy, Francie thought. And weird. Or maybe not that weird since he had studied paleontology.

Forget the bones, she said to herself. She needed to find something that might prove that Redburn was the killer—or at least prove that Theo wasn't.

She spied the file cabinet and strode over to it, skirting a box full of—what were those things—teeth? She had always wanted to rifle through paper files, like detectives do in mysteries, and here was an actual file cabinet, with actual paper files in it.

Going through the As: Antigone, Archaeology articles, Art in Ancient Greece, Francie thought about the conversation she'd just had with her friends, about how Phoebe had not been with the rest of the group. So maybe it was Phoebe who was trying to frame her, Francie thought, in order to cast the blame elsewhere.

Now the Cs: Carpathian, Carpe Diem, Car Insurance . . .

But Phoebe? Strangling Digby? Didn't seem possible. Now that she thought about it, it didn't seem possible that she, Francie, would have been able to strangle Digby either. How could the sheriff even suspect her?

Ah ha! Francie almost shouted. Here was a file marked "Digby"! Score! But maybe, she thought, the sheriff didn't suspect her. Sheriff Warner had to realize that the killer could have only been someone hefty enough to overpower the large, probably very strong Digby. It had to be someone tall and strong . . . like, she thought, sinking once again into despair, Theo.

Or, she thought, as she heard a key turning in the locked office door, *Mr. Redburn.*

19
THE AQUARIUM IN THE WARDROBE

Francie only had time to dart back through the open door into the rack of costumes, pulling the door almost shut behind her before she heard the swoosh of a person entering the office, then footsteps, and keys being set down with a clatter on the desktop.

Crouched behind the door, Francie tried not to move, not to breathe, and, in spite of the prickly fur coat tickling her nose, not to sneeze. Hooking one finger around the edge of the door, she gently and slowly pulled it a little more shut. If she pulled it all the way, it would shut with a click, maybe a clunk. If she pulled too fast, it might be noticed, but if she could pull it slowly enough and get it almost shut, maybe Redburn wouldn't notice it was open.

She stopped when she heard the scrape of his feet growing closer, then pass by, then heard the sound of a file drawer sliding shut.

Silence on the other side of the door made her clamp her lips shut, slowly withdraw her fingers from the edge of the door, and wish like heck she had not assumed this uncomfortable crouching position. Why a crouch? she asked herself. In future hiding situations, remember to take a more comfortable position, and one in which your butt does not fall asleep!

When she heard his distinctive footfall—the limp, she remembered—she let out the breath she had been holding—let it out into the fur coat, which she hoped muffled her exhalation. But the footsteps came closer, while her temples started to throb. It crossed her mind that Raven and Jay knew where she'd gone. If she disappeared from the face of the Earth, at least they would know whom to suspect. But Redburn wouldn't kill her here, would he? I mean, it would be messy—oh, wait, no, he was a strangler—it wouldn't be messy. He could kill her here, wrap her in her own bolt of blue fabric, enshroud her in old costumes . . .

The closet door shut with a click—and a clunk—and Francie sat down with a thump on the floor of the closet, the hems of the fur coats dusting the top of her head.

After her heart resumed its more or less normal rhythm, and her pulse went from 6,500 rpms to idle, she took a deep breath, letting it out slowly—breathing in through her nose and out through her mouth as she'd learned in a yoga-for-acting class, stood up, and realized she was still clutching the Digby file.

She tucked the file into the prodigiousness of her costume— she still hadn't figured out what she was, possibly a circus tent?—and, not hearing anything in the hallway, decided the coast must be clear, so she stepped out into the hall and turned back to make sure the door was locked behind her.

When she turned around again, there was Redburn, standing in the hall.

"Francie?" he said. "I thought you guys were done in there."

"Forgot my phone!" she chirped, a little too brightly. "But I found it. My phone, I mean. It was in there! In the costume shop." *Shut up!* she told herself but heard her mouth running on. "Right where I left it."

Francie tried to avoid looking at him but then remembered that was one of the signs of lying, and so she forced herself to look at his face, at the concerned expression in his brown eyes, which she now noticed were deep and enigmatic. Possibly the kind of look you would have if you were trying to figure out whether someone had just been in your office and stolen a file.

Tipping his head to one side, he said, "What are you supposed to be?"

Be? Did he mean, like, did she fancy herself a sleuth, sneaking around in his office? Was she a bad girl, criminal, vandal, felon?

"Your costume," he clarified. "What is it supposed to be?"

"Oh!" she said, looking down at the oceanic blueness of it. "An aquarium?"

He reached into his pocket while also reaching toward her. She tried not to flinch as he took a length of the drapey fabric in his hands. What was he going to do? Strangle her with her own costume?

But, no, he stuck a couple of colorful fish stickers onto it, and another one on her forehead.

"There you go," he said, putting the sheet of stickers back into his pocket. "Completes the look."

The high school gym had been decorated with orange streamers, orange twinkle lights, and glowing plastic jack-o'-lanterns. There were doughnuts and cider and bobbing for apples. It was all so very … wholesome, or would have been if some of the kids weren't already drunk and others on their way.

Why was she here? Francie wondered, looking over the crowd. Her eyes snagged on a group of girls who had dyed white streaks in their hair, worn in a style like Francie's, not that Francie actually styled her hair. They were even dressed like her, too: black jeans, black top, gray hoodie.

She stared for a moment, then asked Raven, "What's with those girls?" She desperately wanted to get out of there. "Is that their Halloween costume or something?"

"See how popular you are?" Raven said. "The girls are copying you."

"I think maybe they're mocking me."

"No!" Raven laughed. "They're all dressed like cats—you missed the ears and the painted noses and whiskers."

Now that Raven pointed them out, Francie noticed the ears, whiskers, and long tails. "But why the hair?" she said.

"They've been doing that for weeks—you just never noticed."

"Seriously?" Francie asked.

"Seriously," Raven said. "They are copying you."

"Weird."

Francie saw the trench coat and fedora come into the gym. Phoebe. As Francie crossed the room to talk to her, it occurred to her to wonder if it had been Phoebe who had followed her and Theo into Muskie Bait. But why? It didn't make any sense.

"What are you supposed to be?" Phoebe asked when Francie reached her.

"Can't you tell?" Francie pointed to the fish stickers. "An aquarium."

"More like the Atlantic Ocean," Phoebe said, quickly adding, "Kidding!"

"What about you? Is that, like, a detective costume or something?"

"I dunno," Phoebe said. "I just had this stuff that Digby gave me, so I thought I'd wear it."

"Digby gave you that?" Francie said, suddenly very interested.

"So strange," Phoebe said. "He was usually such a turd. Then, at that field trip thing, he just said, 'Hey, you want this? You can use it for Halloween or something.' And handed me this bag of stuff." She shrugged. "Weird."

So, Francie thought, it must have been Digby who chased Theo and me into Muskie Bait! Why? Did Theo know it had been Digby?

While Francie was ruminating, Phoebe pulled the tooth out of the bag and held it up. "What is this, anyway?" she said.

A nearby zombie plucked it out of her hands and tossed it to another zombie who handed it to a devil.

"What the devil is this?" the devil joked, before lobbing it to someone in an ape suit. The tooth went from hand to hand; Francie scrambled after it, trying to intercept it as it was passed like a football, thrown like a softball, and just about to be sent across the floor like a hockey puck when Phoebe hollered in her cheerleading voice, "Stop the madness! Give the nice lady her weird thing!"

The music happened to stop at that precise moment, and everyone in the gym went stone-cold silent as the tooth soared through the air, while Francie simultaneously executed a midair lunge. The partygoers watched, open-mouthed, as the yards of blue fabric in which she was swathed snagged on something and began to unwind.

The tooth splashed down into the punchbowl; Francie made a crash landing on the gym floor; and 8½-by-11-inch white confetti—the contents of the file she'd tucked into the folds of her costume—drifted in the air, then fell to the floor like giant, square snowflakes.

She picked herself up and began hastily gathering papers. Raven, Jay, and a few other people began to help, the band started playing again, and the partygoers returned to their conversations, shouting over the music.

While scooping up the fallen pages, Francie glanced at them and read: "Several counts of felonious smuggling . . . Tyrannosaurus Rex cousin . . . lived seventy million years ago in the Gobi Desert of Mongolia . . . a one-man black market" before she realized that one of the people helping to pick up the papers was Mr. Redburn.

After the pages were retrieved and jammed helter-skelter into their folder, he held out his hand and she handed over the file. She couldn't help but notice what was in his other hand: the tooth, dripping punch.

"My office. Eight a.m. tomorrow morning. Sharp," he said. Without another word, he spun on his heel and disappeared into the depths of the school.

Francie sank into the depths of her ocean-blue costume, now a puddle on the gym floor, a puddle that partygoers did their best to avoid.

It had not been a good day. And things were not looking up.

20
8 A.M.

FRANCIE HAD BARELY SLEPT the night before, and she ran a hand through her hair—as if that were likely to make her seem more alert—before knocking. Despite the lost sleep, she still had not thought up a plausible cover story for why she had that file, how she had gotten it, and why she had been playing football with a Pleistocene-era fossil. The only thing she came up with was: simple answers; don't rattle on. Above all else, don't incriminate Theo. Still, all night, words from the papers on the gym floor rolled around in her brain, especially *smuggling* and *one-man black market* and *Mongolia*. Isn't that where Theo said he'd been, before showing up with a dinosaur tooth in his backpack? Why had he been in Mongolia? Why did Redburn have a file about dinosaur smuggling in Mongolia? Was there some connection?

She steeled herself for whatever was to come: detention, suspension, expulsion—any of which would precipitate a severe scolding from her grandfather. Worse, it might mean a move back to Brooklyn. How did she feel about that? Brooklyn seemed almost boring in comparison to Walpurgis right now. After considering all the possibilities, she put her hand to the door and knocked.

The voice on the other side of the door bid her to enter. As she stepped inside, in spite of her intentions, her eye went immediately to the file drawer. Closed tightly.

Her glance didn't escape Redburn, and he said, "I see you decided to come to my office the normal way this time."

She forced herself to look at her director and couldn't help but notice the tooth resting on its side atop the desk.

"First," he said, "the file. Second, this." He held up the tooth.

Since he hadn't asked her a direct question, she didn't respond.

"What can you tell me about either of those things?" he asked.

What were all the signs of lying, again? All those indications that Jay had talked about? "I don't know?" she tried.

"Why did you take this?" he waved the file at her.

"Curiosity?" she suggested.

"Okay," he said. "That's obvious. Let's cut to the chase. It seems you have taken it upon yourself to do some investigating, in spite of my admonishment and in spite of the sheriff telling you to avoid getting involved—"

"How do you know about that?" Francie broke in. She wasn't going to do that, she reminded herself. She was going to say as little as possible. But, still, how did he know what the sheriff had or hadn't said to her?

"Never mind. I'm assuming you suspect that I might be the murderer—since it was my idea to take a field trip out there the very day of Dr. Digby's death. But if I had wanted to kill Digby, why would I take a pontoon boat full of teenagers along?"

"Cover?" Francie couldn't help but suggest.

He laughed. "Nice theory, but if I've learned one thing, it's that the only thing you can count on teenagers to do is to *not* act the way you want them to."

Francie frowned. "What's that supposed to mean?"

"It wasn't a comment on your acting. I just meant that you can never expect teenagers to do what they're supposed to do in any given situation. Listen, the truth is, the last thing I wanted was Digby dead."

"Why?" Francie said, letting a little sarcasm slip into her voice. "Because you two were such good friends?"

"No, of course not. I'm sure you've figured that out by now."

"Okay," Francie said. "I believe you. I'm sorry I took the file. I was just curious. Why do you have a file on him, anyway?"

Redburn sniffed, glanced down, plucked an invisible piece of lint from his shirt, then looked at her. He seemed to really regard her for a moment.

Francie was ready for anything: a good scolding, which she probably deserved; getting kicked out of the cast, also probably deserved since she still hadn't learned all her lines; being threatened with suspension or at least detention—whatever. Instead, Redburn gestured to the chair on the other side of the desk and told her to sit.

She sat.

"Digby was probably—no, *likely*—involved in fossil theft and smuggling. And . . . hmm . . . how do I put this? Law enforcement agencies are looking into it. But before an arrest could be made, he was murdered. The killer was possibly someone who is also involved in the fossil trade, but so far there's no evidence of that."

Francie's eye flashed on the dinosaur tooth, and she wondered how or if Theo was involved in the fossil trade. But she kept her mouth closed. She hoped Redburn wouldn't ask her how she had come to be in possession of such a thing.

Unfortunately, it was his next question. "How did you come by this?" he asked, placing his hand protectively on the tooth.

"I found it," she said.

"Where?" he asked in a measured tone.

Francie decided she would try to be as honest as possible, but without incriminating Theo. "Muskie Bait," she said.

"You found *this* in Muskie Bait?" Now he sounded incredulous. "For sale, or what?"

"No. It was outside the store. It was stuck in with the teeth, so you'd hardly notice it."

"Yet you noticed it."

"Yeah."

"Just happened to notice it," he repeated.

"Yeah." Keep it simple, she silently reminded herself. Don't rattle on. The more you talk, the more you're likely to slip up.

"Okay," he said. "If you think of anything else you want to share, let me know."

Relieved, Francie rose to go.

"One more thing," he said. She turned toward him.

"Remember when I said, 'Things are not always what they seem'?"

Francie nodded.

"Just keep that in mind," he said.

21

OPENING NIGHT

Sitting in front of the makeup mirror in the girls' dressing room (also the band room), Francie listened with one ear to the conversations going on around her. One of the girls from the chorus was saying that the cold weather they were having proved that global warming was a hoax.

"Yeah, Jenny," Raven said, "because the weather in Walpurgis, Minnesota, pretty much reflects the weather in the entire rest of the world."

Francie let out a little laugh, then went back to being nervous. Opening-night jitters mixed with excitement mixed with worry about Theo mixed with a kind of nausea of not knowing what was going on. It all made a mélange of crunchy, salty, sweet, bitter, and yuck, put into a blender, spun around until reduced to a murky brown sludge, and served to her as a preshow cocktail. Francie knew that once she was onstage, the murk would settle, like mud to the bottom of a pond, and her mind would clear.

Maybe, she thought, applying eyeliner with an unsteady

hand, once her mind cleared, something would make sense. Who could have been the killer?

The interns. It had to be one of the student workers. Had to be! She started painting a line along the lid of her other eye when her phone rang, making her jump, smearing liner all over her eyelid. She picked up her phone with one hand while trying to wipe off the black smudge with the other.

"Hey," Nels said. "Listen, I suppose you're busy right now."

"Uh-huh." Francie closed her left eye and studied the situation in the mirror.

"Sorry I can't come to your show."

"It's okay, Nels. Really, it is." It really was. She was glad he wasn't going to be there. Even though she would love to see him one of these days, she might die of embarrassment if Nels showed up for the play.

"Is your brother going to be there?" he asked.

"Theo?" Francie said. She hadn't even considered the possibility. "No," she said quickly. "Nobody's seen him for days. Weeks, even! The aunts are coming to the matinee on Sunday, but I can't imagine Theo will come." She hadn't allowed herself to think about how she felt about that. Like everything these days, she supposed—mixed.

"Are you worried about him?" Nels asked.

"Theo?" she said again.

"Do you have some other brother?"

"No, I'm not worried about him," she said. "He always does this: appear, disappear, repeat. It's just him."

"Well, anyway, I found out something about the interns— Mallory, Gretchen, Jackson, and Pete," Nels said. "Do you have time for a quick update?"

Francie jammed the eyeliner wand back in the tube and set it down. He had her attention. "What?"

"Turns out that all four of them were grilling and eating burgers at Potter's the night of the murder. Even Mrs. Smattering was there. And they can all vouch for each other."

"For every minute?"

"Apparently. Or at least nobody was out of ear- or eyeshot long enough to have done the deed. They all have watertight alibis," Nels said.

Francie sighed. "Okay."

Bummer. The field was narrowing. Neither Mallory, Gretchen, Jackson, nor Pete could be the killer. Neither could it have been Potter or dear old Mrs. Smattering, not that she was ever a suspect in the first place. And if Redburn was to be believed, it wasn't him, either. Francie did not think Phoebe could have done it. She was too . . . well, other than her lung capacity, she was a flyweight. There just didn't seem like there were any other suspects, except, Francie thought, with ever-increasing desperation, Theo.

Her so-called investigation was supposed to have proved that Theo was not the killer. Instead, what happened was that everything she did, everything she found out, every path she went down just made it seem more and more likely that he was, if not the killer, at least guilty of *something*.

Makeup was applied, hair was knotted into some kind of Grecian-looking do, last-minute touches were made to the costume, places were called, and Francie found herself onstage reciting her lines to Phoebe-as-Ismene.

> *Now dear Ismene, my sister*
> *I cannot imagine any sorrow*
> *That you and I have not gone through. And now—*

Francie continued, at first thinking only of the lines, of herself as Antigone, suffering under the weight of the law, the edict that said her brother's corpse could not be buried. But to not bury him was an affront to the gods! The suffering of Antigone was Francie's, the agony of Antigone's situation Francie felt as her own, the weight of the curse on the house of Oedipus—all this she felt as if she were there, on a dusty Theban street more than two thousand years ago. But when Phoebe-as-Ismene said,

> We are only women,
> Not meant to fight against men

a line that had always irritated Francie, her eye was drawn to the wings, to something out of place. Someone who didn't belong. During Ismene's next lines, Francie squinted past Phoebe into the darkness beyond. Who was that?

ISMENE: *Those who rule are much more powerful.*
We must obey in this . . . and worse.
I will obey those in control.

It was the sheriff, standing in the wings, arms crossed, watching, her eyes not on Phoebe but on Francie. Perhaps Francie should tell the sheriff everything she knew. That was probably the more right thing to do. And no doubt the more legal thing. Would that be for the greater good—the good of society?

ISMENE: *It makes no sense to try to do too much.*

ANTIGONE: *I wouldn't urge you to. No, not even if you*
wanted to.
Be what you want.

They said their lines to each other while Francie's eyes drifted past Phoebe's face. But, unwilling to look at the sheriff, she shifted her gaze out into the house, at the audience. The bright stage lights made it hard to discern any particular person, so her eye drifted confidently over the shadowy figures seated in the auditorium as she said,

I'll still bury him.
I shall lie down
With him in death,

She snagged on the next line when one specific face in the audience was made visible, illuminated by a slightly askew stage light. Theo. She barely choked out the words,

and I shall be as dear to him as he to me. . . .

Lines went by in a blur. Francie apparently said them, although all she could think about was Theo, there in the audience, and the sheriff, there in the wings, and the two of them separated only by a black velveteen curtain.

ISMENE: *Poor Antigone,*
I am so afraid for you!

You should be! Francie thought, her eyes flicking to Phoebe. As Antigone, she said,

Don't fear for me.
You have yourself to consider, after all.

They went on, back and forth, until Ismene said,

You are in love with the impossible.

Francie looked at Phoebe, trying to keep her thoughts on the play but thinking, Isn't everybody in love with the impossible? This is what she was thinking, but she said,

ANTIGONE: *When my strength is gone, I'll give up.*

ISMENE: *Impossible things should not be tried at all.*

What she wanted to say back was, The most worthwhile things to try are the impossible things. And for that matter, Francie thought, the impossible thing is exactly what I am going to try.

The first person Francie ran into when she came off the stage from her scene was the sheriff, who gestured to Francie to step aside before she went for her costume change.

"What is it?" Francie asked.

"I thought you should be made aware, in case you don't understand the gravity of the situation, that withholding evidence in a murder investigation is a felony offense." The sheriff made it sound pretty ominous.

"It sounds like you're suggesting that I'm withholding evidence," Francie said. Her mouth felt dry, but maybe that was from talking so much under hot stage lights. Or maybe it was from having the sheriff standing over her, threatening her with a felony charge. But was it a felony if you withheld evidence during a murder investigation? Or was it during the trial? Even then, it seemed to Francie that it was only in certain circumstances, but she wasn't really sure about all that. Maybe it was true, or maybe the sheriff was trying to frighten her.

"For the moment I am just going to ask you if you know where your brother is."

"Right this minute?" Francie asked.

The sheriff sighed. She took Francie's response, as Francie hoped she would, as a snotty, sarcastic teenager–type response. "No. I mean generally," the sheriff said.

"I don't know," Francie said. This was true. She did not know where Theo was generally. She only knew where he was *right that minute*, which was not what the sheriff wanted to know. She had just said so.

Francie was relieved when the stage manager took her arm and said, "Your costume change, Francie. Hurry!"

. . . . .

At the end of the show, when Francie looked up from the curtain call, Theo was gone. Thankfully, thankfully, gone. The sheriff, Francie saw in a glance, was also gone. She could only hope they did not both go out the same door.

Still shaken from the night's events, she wiped the makeup off her face and reminded herself that, like Antigone, she must try to do the impossible thing. What was the most impossible thing she could try? Proving her brother was not the killer had turned out to be fairly impossible. But something that was impossible to even imagine? Finding her mother. And the answer—irrational, she knew, yet if she didn't allow herself to *think* about it but only to *feel*, it made perfect sense—was to find the silver box.

"You remember we're on our way to Arizona tomorrow, right?" Aunt Jeannette said, as they shared a pizza later.

Francie nodded and said, "Is it okay if I go out to the cabin?"

"I don't think that's a good idea, unless Theo is there," Jeannette said, picking the pepperoni off her slice of pizza.

"Frenchy is perfectly capable of taking care of herself!" Astrid objected. "She hasn't needed her big brother to take care of her these past several years, has she?"

"Let's not get into that!" Jeannette said.

Francie's head ping-ponged from one aunt to the other. She didn't think she'd ever heard them have a spat.

Jeannette turned to Francie. "It will get very cold. You could freeze to death!"

"Oh, for the love of Mike!" Astrid said. "She's too sensible to go freezing herself to death!"

"Well, I don't think she'd do it on purpose!" Jeannette barked.

"She'll be fine." Astrid picked up the rejected pepperoni slices and plunked them on her pizza.

Jeannette heaved a grandmotherly sigh and caved. "Oh, all right," she said. "But you have to know a few things." She proceeded to give Francie a full rundown on the workings of the cabin and finished by saying, "It's not winterized so it's cold in there. Remember that." Then she added, "No parties, no boys. Except Theo, of course, and if Theo's there, then it's okay if there are boys. I suppose he has friends, too."

He doesn't, Francie thought. Wasn't it weird that Theo didn't have any friends? He had never seemed to have any friends, any real ones, even though people seemed to like him. Wasn't it weird that she had never wondered why until now?

Finally, it was Thanksgiving vacation. Francie had declined Nels's invitation to join his family for Thanksgiving. She'd also declined Raven's invitation to "hang out" over the vacation.

"Do you even celebrate Thanksgiving?" Francie'd asked.

"We usually go to a powwow and then eat a big meal—venison, wild rice, squash, maybe even turkey—and then kids watch TV and the grown-ups sit around and complain about white people. I mean, they discuss the injustices indigenous peoples have endured from the time of the pilgrims through the present."

Francie laughed. "Well, sorry to miss it," she said.

She had her own plans: Francie was going to spend the whole time at the cabin. Sandy agreed to give her a ride in his boat after school Wednesday.

Stepping into his speedboat, Sandy said, "Are you sure this is a good idea? How long are you planning to be out here? Is Theo going to be here?"

"Uh-huh," Francie said.

Sandy helped her into the boat and she settled herself into a seat.

"I hope he's bringing the dinner," Sandy said, looking at Francie's little overnight bag. Clearly she'd brought no food. That probably wasn't very smart, she realized.

Sandy tilted his head, studying the bag that in her haste she'd neglected to close up. "What's with the mask and snorkel?" he said. "You're not, like, going to look for that treasure they say is under Enchantment?"

"I thought that was just an old legend," Francie said, zipping up her bag.

"Probably." Sandy started the motor. "But just before he died, my dad said it wasn't just a story."

"What? Really?" Francie couldn't help but sit up and turn toward him.

"Yeah, just before his heart attack he told me that."

"The heart attack you don't really believe was a heart attack," Francie remembered. "You told me that last summer. He died at the hunting shack a few years ago."

"Yeah," Sandy started the motor and pulled the boat away from the dock. "Heart attack or no, whatever it was, it killed him."

"Do you think there's a connection?" Francie had to shout to be heard over the motor as they sped across the lake.

"A connection?"

"I mean, do you think maybe he really discovered something and somebody killed him for it?"

"Oh, gosh!" Sandy said. "No! I never thought that. You really *do* think like a detective, don't you?"

Francie zipped her jacket up as much as she could. Did she think like a detective? She doubted it.

"Well, listen," Sandy went on, "if it stays cold like this, the shallow bays—like where you are—could freeze up pretty good. Might make it hard to get in or out."

"All right, Sandy. I'm just going for a day or two! I'll be fine."

"Is Theo out there already? I haven't seen him lately."

"What is with all the questions?" Francie couldn't keep the exasperation out of her voice.

"Sorry!" Sandy said. "This time of year everything gets a little dicey. You just have to be careful, you know? It's cold. There's ice. I've seen people with hypothermia and it isn't pretty. See? There's ice over here."

He pointed to a thin line of white where the water left off and the translucent sheet of ice began. It crackled as the boat broke through. "See what I mean? It's freezing up already over here."

He gently steered the boat to the shore where the ice was even thicker. "I can't even get up to the shore," he said. "Are you sure you want to do this? Everyone over here has left."

"Yes!" Francie yelped. "I know!"

Sandy helped her step out of the boat onto the shore ice, holding on to her hand a little longer than was necessary, Francie thought. He handed her the overnight bag and her two three-gallon jugs of water—at least she'd thought of that—with obvious reluctance. "Can I help you get a fire going or anything?" he finally said.

"I'll be fine!" Francie said. "I won't do anything stupid. I'm just going to hang out and sleep and rest. It's been a busy fall."

"Okay," Sandy said. "Call if you need anything. Although if the lake freezes up, it'll be hard to get out here for a while. I hope your aunts left you some food!" he called as he pulled away from shore.

Francie nodded and waved as she began the steep ascent to the cabin.

After she'd set her bags down inside and opened the drapes, she carried in some firewood and got a fire going. After heaping blankets on the couch, she climbed under them intending to read for a bit and then go straight to sleep. There was a lot to do the next day. She had a wetsuit, snorkel, mask, and a plan. The next day she would begin looking for that silver box in earnest.

Once she had made herself a little pocket of warmth, sleep came. And with it, dreams of patterned frost, spreading its white fingers over the grass, the cold white lace creeping from the grass onto her feet, spreading up her legs and over her whole body, slowly seeping into her skin and freezing her from the outside in . . .

She woke shivering, the blankets having slipped off during the night. Frozen and forlorn, she thought. No heavenly smell of cinnamon rolls, no cheery "Good morning!" from the kitchen. It was really quiet. Unusually quiet. Even considering the lack of aunts.

What was it she wasn't hearing?

She climbed out of bed and quickly pulled on her wool socks and her parka, flipping the hood up. Once she got the fire going again, she looked out the picture window at the lake. It was very still. Still, as they say, as glass.

The thing she had not been hearing, she realized, was water. No waves lapping against the shore, no ducks beating their wings on the surface of the lake. Nothing. The lake was no longer composed of moving water; it was covered over by a skin of ice. All except way out in the middle, where there was the shimmer of water.

Her phone rang. She'd have to remember to turn it off after this call to save the battery.

"Are you at the cabin?" Jeannette asked.

"Yep," Francie answered. "There's ice on the lake!"

"Oh my!" Astrid chirped, adding, "We have you on speaker-phone!"

"Is Theo there?" Jeannette asked.

"Nope," Francie said. She wondered again, Where was he? Why wasn't he here?

"How did you get there?"

"Sandy gave me a ride over in his boat yesterday. There wasn't so much ice then. He said to call when I want to get back, and he'd come and get me."

"You might not get out of there for a while. Until it either breaks up or freezes hard enough to walk on," Jeannette said. "Don't you dare try walking on it! If you need to get back, call Sandy."

"Uh-huh." Francie strolled into the kitchen. She opened a cupboard to find it mostly, like Mother Hubbard's, bare.

"Did you bring any food with you?" Astrid asked.

"Sure . . . ," Francie said. She hadn't, but neither she nor they could do anything about that now, so she didn't see any point in bringing it up.

"Are you going to be all right by yourself?"

"Uh-huh."

There was a pause, and then Jeannette said, "Don't walk any-where on the ice! There are springs and currents and things, and even when the ice seems safe, it isn't necessarily so."

"Right-o." Francie opened another mostly bare cupboard. "I'll be fine. Don't worry!"

After scrounging up a breakfast of stale crackers and instant coffee in not quite hot enough water (due to impatience), Francie put on her jacket, boots, hat, and mittens and walked through the woods to the Fredericksons' house.

Except for the crunch of frosty leaves underfoot, it was quiet.

All the cabins were closed up, their windows shuttered, the curtains drawn. Lawn furniture had been put away; docks were stacked along the shore. Far out on the lake, Francie could hear the comical tooting of a flock of trumpeter swans, honking away like the eighth-grade cornet band.

At last she arrived at the Fredericksons', about the most forlorn of all of the places in spite of its elegance, because it had been so neglected since last July. She followed a silvery path of flattened grass, she supposed made by some animal, down to the shore. "How could you do this?" she accused the lake. "How could you freeze *now*, when I finally had a chance to really look?"

As if in response, the ice let loose a long, shivery crackle.

The ice was not thick enough to walk on, but it certainly presented an obstacle to swimming. She shivered thinking about that. How did she think she was going to do this? Did she really think a wetsuit was going to do the trick? That water temperature was somewhere in the vicinity of thirty-two degrees. She wasn't going in there—it was insane. It really was an impossible thing, and maybe Ismene was right: impossible things should not be attempted at all. Lest you freeze to death!

Maybe by tomorrow the wind would come up and push the ice away, and she could take the canoe out there. That seemed like a rational plan, and she would have been pleased if only she didn't have the disconcerting feeling that she was not alone. As she walked back toward the cabin, she couldn't keep herself from glancing over her shoulder every now and then. When from behind her she heard the distinct crack of a twig, she spun around, heart thumping, and peered into the forest. Don't get all hysterical, she told herself. If someone was following me, I would be able to see that person, because the branches are bare of leaves. Wouldn't I?

But there—had she seen something just now, something ducking behind that cabin?

Francie ran the rest of the way to the cabin, flung open the door, rushed inside, closed the door behind her, and threw the deadbolt.

"A restorative cup of tea is what I need," she said out loud, remembering a line from some British show she'd seen. She found a stash of tea and put a pot of water on the stove. "And something to eat." That might be more difficult.

A thorough scouring of the cupboards turned up a box of Minute Rice, some pasta, a small tin of sardines forgotten in the back of a cupboard—generally canned goods weren't left behind as their contents expanded and sometimes burst when frozen. And—oh, goodie!—a cookie jar full of forgotten Oreos. Perhaps forgotten since the 1980s, but she was not going to be fussy at a time like this.

Once the water boiled and the tea was made, Francie sat down to her Thanksgiving dinner: sardines, Oreos, and tea. And tried not to feel sorry for herself. This was her own doing, after all. She had refused invitations from Nels and from Raven. The aunts had gone to Arizona. Theo . . . who knew? And she had wanted to be alone.

Or so she'd thought.

Now she regretted it. It would be nice to be with Nels, maybe to meet his family, although that was a little scary. I mean, she thought, are Nels and I that serious? He was in college, but she was still only in high school. It's not like they were going to get married or anything!

At least she felt better now with a little something in her stomach and the tea, which had indeed been restorative. She laughed at herself for being spooked, but residual fear clung to her like frost.

At the fireplace, Francie poked at the coals, then piled on the last of the wood—she'd have to get more before bed—then decided to look around the place for anything that might reveal something about her mother. Without her aunts around, she could really do some earnest snooping.

The photo albums were first: here was a picture of herself with Theo in a canoe. Here, wearing funny hats, picking raspberries. They had been close when they were younger, she remembered. She had looked up to him.

Why were there no photos of her mother? That's what she wanted to know. Had her mother been so terrible that every trace of her had been destroyed? What had she done? Wouldn't her aunts have kept at least one photo of her?

Yes. Francie was sure they would, and it was somewhere in this house. She felt like a detective as she hunted through drawers and cupboards and ran her hands under folded clothing. Or maybe, she thought, as she pawed through boxes and bins and flung open closet doors, she was behaving more like a burglar.

Finally, she opened an old trunk of Astrid's. The scent of mustiness, old wool, and a little wisp of mystery rose from the box. Beneath some moth-eaten sweaters and an old tennis racket (she tried and failed to picture Astrid on a tennis court), she came upon an ancient yellowed newspaper lining the bottom of the trunk. Really old! she thought, taking a closer look. The story, dated June 1930, was about a gangster bootlegger who ran a liquor-smuggling operation in the area. "Invisible Bill," they called him, because he seemed to disappear into thin air whenever the Feds came around. The liquor had been smuggled into the U.S. from Canada, the story said, but so far the operators remained at large.

Francie gently pried the newspaper off the bottom of the trunk and flipped it over. A photograph of the man in question made her rock back on her heels. He had a white streak in his hair, exactly like hers! And like her mother's.

That was creepy. And it was uncanny. And there was only one explanation: she was related to this gangster. So her ancestors had been bootleggers? In other words, criminals. This did not surprise her. It just confirmed what she had long suspected. But did that mean she herself was doomed to a life of crime? She thought of all the lying she had done lately and felt pretty darned doomed.

Francie was about to shut the trunk when she noticed something else, something that had been hidden under the newspaper: a small, locket-sized photograph. She picked it up and squinted at it—daylight was fading and she had yet to light the kerosene lamps. Still, she knew it was her mother the minute she looked at it. There was an eerie similarity to herself, made more distinct by the white streak in her mother's hair—just like her own. And just like the gangster's in the newspaper.

Taking the small photograph, Francie walked into the living room, set the photo on the coffee table, and lit the kerosene lamps and a few candles for good measure. Then she sat down on the couch and stared at the photo. Stared and stared. There was her mother. Francie tried to call her to mind, but she had been too little when her mama had . . . what? The official story was that she died, and Francie had the story memorized for anyone who asked her.

But she had never believed it. Why? Her father had died in a car accident, and she never had trouble believing that—although she didn't believe it was an accident as they said. But her mother, according to Theo, was still alive . . . somewhere.

She turned her gaze away from the photo and toward the window. Night had fallen and what she saw instead of the lake was her reflection in the glass, looking very much like the photo in her hand. It was almost as if she might be seeing her own mother on the other side of the window. Then the visage changed somehow, eerily, into a ghostly face quite unlike her own that hovered just outside the window before moving away.

What had she just seen? Had that been some trick of reflection? Of imagination? Of darkness? Of hunger? The ghost of Invisible Bill? Or was there an actual person out there?

Francie cupped her hands against the window glass to shut out the background light and peered into the darkness.

Nothing.

She shivered, then glancing at the dying embers in the fireplace, thought of the empty woodbin.

"Oh, crap!" she cried. The fire would die soon and she'd neglected to carry in any split wood or logs from the woodpile. She couldn't spend all night in the cabin without a fire—she'd be as frozen as a polar bear's toenails!

She threw on her jacket and a headlamp and went outside, pausing for a moment on the stoop to listen, before switching on the headlamp. As she strained to hear any little sound, her eyes scanned the dark woods and she slowly made her way to the woodpile.

Once there, she piled on as much wood as she could carry and hoped like heck it would be enough to last through the night. She sure wasn't coming out here again in the dark.

Inside, she dumped the load of kindling and logs in the woodbin, then reached for a few smaller sticks to get the fire going. But just before she put the kindling on the fire, she stopped and stared at the stick in her hand. The "stick" was not a stick. It was, it slowly dawned on her, a bone. A *human* bone.

22

UNDER ENCHANTMENT

FAINT LIGHT GLIMMERED in the sky when she woke. The fire was out and it was so cold that Francie's breath made puffs of white steam at every exhale. She got up, dragging the coverlet with her as she went to the fireplace and got the fire going again.

The bone she'd found lay somewhere outside where she'd tossed it the night before. Now, in the daylight, she just laughed. Of course it was an animal bone! Why had she ever thought it was from a human? Only because she'd been so spooked. How would she even know a human bone from an animal bone? She wouldn't!

"What a baby," she scolded herself. "Somebody's dog probably dragged that thing out of the woods and left it on our woodpile. A dog with a morbid sense of humor."

After a breakfast of instant coffee—sadly, no cream, milk, or anything white to put in it—and the last of the sardines, she bundled up, took a handful of Oreos, and went out to check the ice. She barely glanced at the bone that lay among the fallen leaves outside the cabin.

By the time she got to the Fredericksons', the Oreos were gone. The ice was not. In fact, if anything, it looked thicker, more solid. Francie picked up a stone and tossed it, watching it ping and bounce along the ice. She tried it with a bigger stone, then a fist-size rock, then a two-hander. All the rocks remained securely on top, which seemed encouraging, so she took a tentative step onto it, then another, then another—far enough to realize that the ice had frozen perfectly clear. It was like an enormous picture window with a spectacular view of the bottom of the lake.

It seemed pretty solid. If she fell through, she'd only get her feet wet, so she might as well give it a try. So far, so good. A few more steps. Still solid! She could tell by the cracks in the ice how thick it was, and she remembered that to support a person you only need, like, what, a couple of inches? Francie minced along, mostly because it was so eerie to walk on such clear ice.

The cracks and fissures in the ice were black, but sunlight illuminated the bottom so that it was like looking down on the ruins of an underwater city: pale rocks strewn like the toppled remains of a wall, waterlogged driftwood scattered like animal bones, and here and there the glint of clamshells, bright as china plates. And under her feet, darting fish.

Entranced, she paid little attention to where she was going, just staring through the ice at the bottom below.

Her phone rang. It was Raven. She needed to remember to turn it off to save the battery.

"The lake froze," she said.

"No way!" Raven said.

"But Raven," Francie's voice was hushed, "it's like glass. It's completely translucent."

There was a pause. "Frenchy? Are you out on it?"

"Not very far," Francie said. "Just a few steps."

"Listen to me. Don't go out on it."

"Yeah, yeah, I know," Francie said. "The aunts have already given me the lecture. But remember how shallow it is here, and for quite a ways? So even if I did bust through, I'd be able to stand up. How bad could *that* be?"

"Bad," Raven said. "Really bad." When Francie didn't respond, Raven said, "Frenchy?"

"I'll call you back." Francie hung up and put the phone in her pocket. She had seen something at the bottom of the lake. It was as if she were looking through a window at it: some silver thing half buried in sand—a silver square that almost seemed to emit a pulsing glow. She stared at it for a long moment, thinking, I didn't imagine it. I'm not going bonkers. That must be it—what else could it be? She howled like a coyote, first with happiness, then with frustration.

"The box is under the ice," she cried and, kneeling, pounded her fists on the ice. "Under!" (*Pound!*) "The!" (*Pound!*) "Ice!" (*Pound pound pound!*)

She lay down, cupped her hands around her eyes, and stared down at it. "Far, far away there is a lake," she said. "On the lake there is a sheet of ice. Under the ice there is water. Under the water there is the bottom. On the bottom there is a box. In the box there lies my heart."

The sand sloped down into inky darkness, and she realized she was looking at the edge of the drop-off. There were deep spots in this lake, she remembered, 180 feet at the deepest. If the box had landed just a few inches farther out, she'd never have spotted it. It might have been impossible to ever find it.

Her chest felt tight when she realized how easily the box could slip over that edge, pushed by currents or wind. Or it could easily become completely buried under the sand. She'd have to retrieve it as soon as possible. "Okay, think," she muttered to herself, "mark the spot." She slid a mitten off her hand, laid it on the ice, then stood and looked back toward the shore, noticing how the shadows lay from this angle and marking where she was between those two pines. That's when she noticed something else. There was someone—a person—standing mostly behind a tree but not quite entirely. Watching her.

How long had that person been there, following her movements? Where had he come from? How long had he been there, watching her?

Now she was out here, exposed and vulnerable, while he was in the shadows of the trees. Did he know she'd seen him?

Francie started walking away, not toward shore where the person was watching, but on the ice toward her aunts' cabin. She sensed the shadowy figure following her, but along the shore. If she glanced landward, she could just discern movement in and out of the trees. He was lagging a little behind, like a wolf, Francie thought, following a wounded deer. No, she thought, not quite that. There was something wrong with that metaphor . . .

This is what she was thinking when the ice gave way under her.

23
SLEEP AT LAST

IT WAS NOT LIKE FALLING INTO WATER. It was beyond cold, beyond wet. It was like plunging into mercury or being seared by liquid nitrogen or some other completely unfamiliar element.

The thing to do, her mind screamed while her arms and legs churned the water, was . . . *get out!* She tried to obey, tried to fling herself up on the sheet of ice, but she barely got her arms on top of it when it gave way under her, only widening the hole. She tried getting a grip on the ice with her fingernails, but the ice was too slick and her fingernails too short.

Get out! her mind ordered again.

But she could make no effort to do it. Her limbs were so numb they wouldn't obey. Then yell for help, she told herself, but when she tried, the sound strangled in her throat like a scream in a nightmare.

The sun had burnished the ice into something metallic look-ing—a stainless steel countertop, like the kind in a morgue. *Good-bye to the sun that shines for me no longer,* she thought. Or perhaps she said it. Lines from the play darted in and out of her mind like minnows: *Now sleepy Death summons me down . . . down . . .* water dragged her down. Water, thick and black as oil, oil from fossils, fossils from bones, bones from dragons, dragons from underground. *Soon I shall be with my own again . . . . And I shall see my father again, and you, mother . . . passing to that chamber where all find sleep at last.*

24
WARM

THE FACT THAT SHE FELT WARM probably meant she was nearly dead. Wasn't that how it was? You started to feel warm and that was the beginning of the end. Did she dare open her eyes? It was too frightening to think about, to imagine the darkness, the emptiness, the impossibility of escape. But she had to know, so she opened them . . . and found herself in a room, on a bed, under a blanket. No, under about ten blankets. Blankets she recognized, a bed she recognized, in a cabin she recognized.

"Hello, you're awake," said Theo, stepping into the room.

Francie tried to sit up but felt herself dragged down by the weight of the blankets and something heavy in her head. Her mind seemed to be like a bad TV channel, mostly static and white fuzz. In there somewhere something was trying to come into focus.

"Theo!" she said. "When did you get here?"

"Just in the nick of time, apparently," he said.

"Did you pull me out of the lake?"

He looked around as if to say, Do you see anyone else around here? "What you were doing in the lake, anyway?" he asked. "Just going for a dip?"

How had Theo gotten here? Francie wondered. He hadn't been at the cabin, so where had he come from? He couldn't have come across the ice—as was demonstrated, it really wasn't safe—so where had he come from and why had he been there and found her at that precise moment? It was all so odd and kind of creepy, and she felt so woozy and dizzy, she couldn't seem to formulate the words to ask.

Something had come to her while she'd been unconscious—or whatever she'd been. She'd had a flash—or flashes—of insight. But trying to find them again . . . it was as slippery as trying to remember a dream.

"Francie!" Theo waved his hand in front of her face. "Hello?"

"I just went out on the ice a ways to look at the bottom—it was so clear! And then a little farther and a little farther—I didn't realize I'd gone out so far."

"When I saw you, you seemed to be hurrying right along."

"How did you happen to be . . . why were you around to save me?"

"Raven called and told me you were out here and she was a little worried about you. No, a lot worried." He turned, glanced back, and then rushed out, calling over his shoulder, "I've got something on the stove."

Francie could smell something cooking in the kitchen. Something good.

"What did she say?" she called after Theo. She heaved off the blankets, lunged out of bed, and staggered into the living room. Her boots were propped up near the fireplace where a cheery fire was burning, and her jacket and other clothes hung from the rafters.

"Planning on going somewhere?" Theo leaned against the door frame holding a mug of something steaming. He put the mug into her hands and said, "Drink this."

Francie sank down on the couch, sipped on the warm cocoa, and tried to sort through what had been a dream and what had happened in the moments after she'd fallen through the ice. "How long do you think I was in the water before you pulled me out?"

"You're welcome, by the way," Theo said, sitting down next to her.

"Oh, Theo," Francie said. "I'm sorry. Didn't I say thank you?" She flung her arms around him. "Thank you for saving my life, you big, frilly, apron-wearing lug." She slugged him, but not very hard. "You smell like Aunt Jeannette."

"We use the same aftershave," Theo said, getting up and going back into the kitchen.

Francie laughed a little and looked back out the window, squinting at the brightness. "What did Raven say to you?"

"She just said that if I had a way to get out here, maybe I should come. Good thing I did, huh?"

"How did you get here?"

"Canoe—stick a foot out and scoot the canoe along on the ice until you hit open water, then paddle. Etcetera. What are you doing out here? Trying to solve the murder?"

"No!" Francie said. "I—no. I'm not trying to solve any murders. I don't want to be some sort of stupid northwoods Nancy Drew."

"All right, then, Nancy. I mean, Francie," he said.

She threw a pillow at him; he caught it midair and said, "Now I know why they call these things *throw pillows*," then threw it back at her. "So, are you going to tell me what you were doing on the ice?"

"What about you?" Francie said. "You haven't explained anything. Like where you've been. Or how you knew Digby and what you two were arguing about. Or tell me why you came here. Or explain what you know about—"

"Okay, okay," he said. "What do you want to know first?"

For a moment the static cleared and it seemed as if the plunge under the ice had scoured Francie's mind into a kind of shiny silver platter, ready to receive anything in a cool, detached way. All other queries paled next to the one brightly polished question on that platter: "Mom?" she asked.

"Okay," Theo said. "But remember, once you know something, you can't unknow it, and in this case, it is a secret you have to keep from everyone. *Everyone.* You can't even tell Raven," he said. "You should also know that once you know a big secret, a secret you can't share with anyone, you can't avoid lying. In fact, in a way, your whole life becomes a lie."

"You've said that," she said. She didn't add that she had also come to understand what he'd meant by it.

Theo walked back into the kitchen. Francie could hear him chopping something, and she followed him in.

"You are stalling," she said. "And where did you get vegetables? Did you bring groceries?"

"I was just leaving the grocery store when Raven called."

"You said that Mom had stolen something. Were you telling me that our mother is a thief?"

"That's one possibility."

"So the other possibility is that she isn't?"

"Right. She may very well have been saving a priceless antiquity from falling into nefarious hands. She was most likely keeping it from the smugglers. But what happened was that everyone went after her: the smugglers, yes, but also the agency that she worked for and the CIA as well as international intelligence agencies."

"Geez!" Francie said. "So she's like Jason Bourne."

"Who?" Theo said.

"You are so out of it! Where have you been?"

"This is what I've been doing with my life. Looking for Mom. For the past two years I've devoted every waking minute to finding her."

A lump formed in Francie's throat. She had been so convinced that Theo had just been throwing away his trust money by gallivanting around the world having adventures . . . and all this time, he'd been looking for their mother. Francie rubbed her forehead, shielding her eyes with her hand. She didn't want him to see that she was crying.

"But this is why she had to disappear—completely disappear. And why it was important that none of us in the family knew anything. If we didn't know where she was, we couldn't say. It was a form of protection for all of us. Otherwise, we would be in danger, too."

A little thrill poured through Francie, a thrill mixed with a kind of carbonated excitement, with a squeeze of lime. Maybe their mother was not a criminal. "Things are not as they seem," she said, remembering Redburn's words.

"What?" Theo said.

"Nothing," Francie answered. "But . . . so you're saying that nobody can find her: not the organization she worked for, not the CIA, not the smugglers . . . but *you're* going to find her?"

"Well, not me *alone*," Theo said.

"Who are you working with?"

"I'm hoping to work with you," Theo said. "That is, if you can keep yourself alive long enough."

Francie kind of laughed. Really, she didn't know what else to do.

"The thing is," he went on. "I've been all over the world: South America, the Middle East, Asia, Mongolia, learning things little by little, and you know where my investigation led me?"

"Here," Francie offered.

"Yeah," Theo said. "Right here."

Time seemed to stop for a moment. Had there been the ticking of a clock, the hum of a refrigerator, the buzz of a fan, this would have been the moment when Francie would have been aware of those sounds. But there was nothing. Silence.

Then Theo said, "You tell me what you were doing out on the ice, and I'll tell you everything else." He turned back to his vegetables.

Francie whined and pleaded, then hemmed and hawed, but finally got out about the silver box, where it had been, how she had seen it disappear into the lake, and that she'd gone out on the ice to find it. "I remember it from when I was little," she told him, "but then it disappeared at some point. Still, I kind of always remembered it and started thinking of it as the place where I kept my heart. I know it doesn't make any sense, and is weird and everything, but it was a kid thing."

Theo, she realized, had stopped chopping. He stood with his hands on the countertop, his back to her. He was very still.

"Theo? I know it was weird, but—"

"Go on," he said.

She told him about seeing it at the Fredericksons' and finally going with Raven to look for it, but how it wasn't there. Instead, someone else was there, and she thought that person had also been looking for the box and had taken it and for some reason had thrown it in the lake. She knew she was right about that because she had seen it—had seen the box under the ice right before she fell in.

"Frenchy, why didn't you tell me?"

"Tell you what?"

"About the box."

"You would have just told me to leave it alone, to forget about it, it was in my imagination, to stop obsessing about Mom—I don't know! All the things you've always said when I bring up anything having to do with her. There's another reason, too," Francie said softly. "You have a secret. You have a lot of secrets, it seems to me, and I didn't see any reason to confide in you when I don't, I can't, trust you."

"You can't trust me? Why not?"

"For all I know you're a murderer!" she blurted out.

As soon as she said it, she regretted it. What if he was a murderer? And if he wasn't, what a terrible thing to say to your own brother!

He had turned and now he looked at her, his face a study in disbelief. "Why would you think that?" he said.

"I heard you arguing with Digby. You were gone during the time he was murdered. I saw you washing your hands in the lake."

Theo laughed. "I'd been gathering mushrooms for dinner, you goof."

"Mushrooms? I don't remember any mushrooms."

"They were overlooked in all the excitement. When I got back to the cabin, you and the aunts were on the phone to the sheriff's office, and I just set the mushrooms in the kitchen. I think they were forgotten."

"Oh," Francie said. How stupid she'd been. Why hadn't she just asked?

"As for Digby, yes, I did argue with him. I didn't really know him. I just knew who he was."

"I guess he was kind of famous," Francie said, "as archaeologists go. So if he was such a hotshot, why was he here digging up dime-a-dozen mastodon bones?"

"Exactly," Theo agreed. "I think he was trying to get out of the limelight, because he was the director of a dig—a big one, potentially very big—when something major went missing from the site. What's not clear is whether he was involved or not."

"Was it the world's biggest dinosaur?" Francie guessed.

Theo squinted at her out of one eye. "You figured that out?"

"Well, not so much me as Jay," Francie admitted. "But, anyway, you came here to talk to Digby. You didn't come here to see me or to tell me about Mom, or any of that." Francie's gut felt like a garbage disposal full of emotions, all grinding away in there.

"Well, it's complicated," Theo protested. "But, see, it's all tied together somehow."

"So why were you arguing with Digby?"

"I asked him what he was doing here. He flew off the handle, just lost it. He was so defensive about it, I figured the rumors must be true."

"What rumors?"

"That there is something else around here that he was really looking for. Something bigger."

"Bigger than mastodon bones?"

"Not literally bigger, but more important. A big find. Possibly huge."

"Like what? Wait a minute," Francie lowered herself onto the couch. "You're talking about the treasure, aren't you? That old legend?"

"It might not be just a legend," Theo said.

"Funny," Francie mused. "Sandy said the same thing just

the other day. He said that his dad told him that it wasn't just a legend. That was just before he . . . died."

Theo and Francie looked at each other.

"But, Theo," Francie said, "what is it? What is the treasure? And where is it?"

Theo swallowed. "The answer," he said, "is in that silver box."

25
THE SITUATION

"I'M GOING TO GO check out the situation," Theo said, pulling on his boots. "You stay here."

"NO! I have to show you where it is," Francie insisted. But as soon as she had pulled on her dry socks—nice and warm from the fire—she felt a pang of worry. She stared into the fire for a moment, trying to think.

"Sure you're okay?" Theo asked, his brows knit with concern.

"Yeah," she rubbed her forehead. "Fine."

"Look," Theo said. "I'm just checking on the thickness of the ice over there, that's all. You stay here. You're not recovered yet. And you don't want to get pneumonia."

There was something about the plan Francie didn't like, but she was still so foggy that she couldn't put her finger on what it was. "I wish you wouldn't," was all she could think to say.

"Stir the soup," Theo commanded as he threw on his jacket. "I'm not going to do anything dangerous." Then he added, just before going out the door, "Don't worry."

But Francie was worried. Why? *He's just going over to assess the situation,* she told herself. Still, there was something niggling at her, something that felt just out of reach—like trying to remember a dream after waking.

She wandered into the kitchen and lifted the lid on the soup, breathing in the steam and heavenly aroma. When had Theo learned to cook? There was so much she didn't know about him, and now she was sorry that she'd avoided him when she could have gotten to know him better. He might go away again anytime. And if he did, she might never finish hearing about her mother. Why, she wondered now, as she stood stirring the soup, had she not demanded to hear the rest of the story before he went out? Why was she always so willing to be distracted or to get off track when it came to her mother?

It's because she was afraid. Afraid to know. But what was she so afraid of? She would ask Theo, she would! It's the first thing she would do, she decided, right after she ate some soup. She scooped out a bowlful and, careful not to slosh, carried it to the couch where she sat slurping and eating. The veggies were still pretty crunchy, but she didn't care—it felt as if she hadn't eaten for days. Well, she thought, she hadn't! No wonder she was so hungry.

"I should slow down," she said out loud, "and not wolf this down."

As soon as she said the word *wolf,* something flashed in her mind, like a snippet of a remembered dream—the image of a wolf trailing a deer.

She set her bowl down on the coffee table. The old fear returned. Fear for Theo. What was it?

A wolf stalking a deer.

Then it came to her: before she fell through the ice, she'd seen someone, someone watching her, and that person trailed her as she walked on the frozen lake. She'd felt like a wounded deer being trailed by a wolf. Or something like that.

Someone else was here, here on this side of the lake.

Then she remembered the face in the window. The bone on the log pile.

Things she had forgotten to tell Theo.

She had to go after him.

But her clothes were still wet. Steam rose from her boots, propped up by the fireplace. Her jacket was sodden. Well, the aunts had clothes, she thought, and she went into the closet to see what she could find. Once she was more or less bundled up, she set off, lumbering along as best she could in a pair of oversized boots and a too-big jacket.

When Francie arrived at the shore in front of the Fredericksons' the word that popped into her head was *vandalized*. The ice had been crudely chopped through, broken and frayed at the edges. Bright shards and glittering bits on the shore lay scattered like broken glass. And there was a big round gaping hole in the ice right where Francie had seen the silver box.

Something on the ground caught her eye: a full wetsuit, mask, and snorkel spread out in the grass as if the person wearing these things had lain down and then dissolved into oblivion.

Someone else had been here, and Theo had either come upon whoever it was or had gone to find that person. Or something worse had happened.

It didn't take long to find him. As Francie continued down the path, she saw him lying, an inert lump, on the ground.

Francie ran, or rather gallumphed in her big boots, to where he lay. Her breath caught somewhere it didn't belong—neither lungs nor throat, but somewhere outside herself, and she found it hard to choke out the word, "Theo?"

He groaned; his eyes flickered open; he said, "Oh, my head," which made Francie laugh.

"I don't see what's so funny." Theo looked at her through pain-narrowed eyes.

"I'm relieved, is all," she said, trying to squash a giggle. No use—it burbled out. "I thought you were dead."

"That's pretty hilarious, all right," he said and let out a little snorting laugh, so she knew he really was okay. Still, when he sat up, he yelped in pain.

"What happened?" Francie asked, eyeing the lump rising on his head.

"Someone bashed me from behind. I didn't see who it was."

Francie glanced up and cast her eyes in every direction, peering through the woods. The assailant had to be here somewhere. "There!" she whispered, pointing at movement glimpsed through the trees. There was something familiar about the movement, something that made her feel cold to her very hair follicles.

That gait—that strange, uneven way of walking—the limping wolf. It came to her: the reason the analogy of the wounded deer trailed by a wolf had been wrong is that it had been the *wolf* who had seemed wounded—because of its limp, its strange gait.

"Not moving real fast," Theo whispered. "Let's just stay back and try to stay out of sight. See where he's going."

They set off, staying well behind, catching only glimpses of the fleeing figure. Near the old shack—the same place Francie had come to the night of the murder—Theo ducked behind a tree and motioned to Francie to do the same. From their hiding spot, they watched as the figure disappeared into the shack.

"You stay here. I'm going in," Theo whispered.

"If you're going in, I'm going in." Francie crossed her arms belligerently.

"All right, then," Theo agreed. "Let's go."

The place was empty. That was immediately apparent.

"We saw someone come in here," Theo said, scratching the stubble on his chin.

"Yeah, and there's no other door. There's no other way out. We would have had to see him come back out, right? But creepy!" Francie eyed the box of graham crackers sitting open on the table. Candles, a flashlight. Sleeping bag on the bed. Soap in the sink. A towel. A pitcher of water. "Somebody's been staying here!" she whispered.

These past couple of days, she'd thought she'd been alone on this side of the lake. But this explained why she felt she'd been followed. It explained the face at the window. But it didn't explain how whoever had come in here had gotten out without being seen.

Theo checked the windows. "All latched from the inside," he said. He lifted a foot and looked at the sole of his shoe. "Sticky," he said.

"Yeah," Francie agreed, listening to her shoes go *shkk-shkk* when she walked.

Continuing his search, Theo moved a chair, looked under the table, went to the single, doorless closet hung with a couple of flannel shirts and peeked inside.

"No place to hide," Francie said.

"There's got to be some way we don't know about. Unless this person can just turn invisible!"

"Like Invisible Bill," Francie said.

"Who?"

"This old bootlegger who had some kind of hideout around here and was never caught. They called him Invisible Bill because he just seemed to disappear. Also, I think he was related to us."

"Why do you think that?"

"Had one of these." Francie pointed to the white streak in her hair. "And it happened here. On Enchantment. Federal agents would chase him, surround his hideout, and he would just—*poof!*—disappear."

"Do you think this might have been the place?"

Francie shrugged. "I don't know."

"Well, we better try to be smarter than those federal agents." Theo kicked at a throw rug on the floor. "Weird," he said.

"What?" Francie came up behind him.

"This rug doesn't move," he said. "It's like glued to the floor or something." Theo lifted the edge of the rug to peek underneath. Francie retrieved the flashlight from the table and shone the beam under the rug, where there appeared to be a crack in the floor.

"Maybe they glued the rug down to keep the mosquitoes out."

"Or maybe—" Theo lifted the rug and part of the floor with it.

"The rug is covering a trapdoor!" Francie exclaimed. She aimed the light down into the dark hole. "It seems deep," she said, peering into the gloom. "How far do you think it goes down? Is it a kind of root cellar, do you think? Or . . . is this how Invisible Bill disappeared?"

"More to the point," Theo said, "is this how our mystery person disappeared?" He took the flashlight from Francie and focused the light down the hole, revealing a ladder leading into the inky darkness. "Only one way to find out," he said.

At the bottom of the ladder they found themselves in a kind of underground chamber with enough room to walk around. But no sign of anyone.

The flashlight beam illuminated rows of plastic barrels lining one of the walls.

"Whoa! What're those?" Francie said. "Bootlegged whiskey?"

"They didn't have plastic barrels back in the 1920s and '30s. These are much newer. Brand-new, I'd say."

"What do you suppose is in there?" Francie wondered.

"Can't tell," Theo said. The beam played over a wooden cupboard that stood against another wall. The door only needed a nudge to swing open with a creak—to reveal nothing.

"The cupboard is bare," Theo pointed out.

"This gets weirder and weirder," Francie said. "We saw someone go inside and didn't see anyone leave."

"Whoever it is must have gotten out of the cabin some other way," Theo mused. "Let's go look again." He started up the ladder. "Maybe there's something we missed."

While Theo was climbing the ladder, Francie took another look around.

"You coming?" he said, shining the flashlight down toward her. The beam bounced off the walls and along the barrels and suddenly snagged on something. A small thing sitting on one of the barrels. Something that gave off a dull gleam.

"Theo . . . ," Francie said.

But Theo didn't answer. The door above slammed shut and Francie was plunged into complete darkness. Worse than complete darkness—*underground* darkness. Overhead, she could hear footsteps and what sounded like something heavy being dragged across the floor.

"Theo?" she called. "Theo!" Francie scrambled up the ladder and pressed on the hatch. It wouldn't budge. She put her shoulder to it and pushed as hard as she could. "The-o-dore Frye! This. Is. Not. Funny!"

What had just happened? She felt that dizzying fear again—

not for herself, for Theo. Theo would not have shut the hatch on her. That meant someone must have intercepted him.

Francie had no way out! Not even any light because Theo had taken the flashlight. But then she remembered that before the flashlight had disappeared, it had shone its light on something they hadn't noticed before.

She climbed back down the ladder and groped along the barrels until her hand bumped against something different. She knew immediately what it was: a box, *the* box, the *silver* box.

"Theo!" she cried. "Thee-ohhhh!"

Pressing the box against her chest, she slumped against one of the damp walls of the underground room, not caring what kind of green slime she got on her clothes. The silver box was in her hands!

Wasn't it ironic, she thought, that she finally got what she'd been longing for all her life, the box that was going to lead her to her mother, and now Francie was going to die, succumbing to hypothermia or being buried alive, whichever came first?

The cold from her earlier plunge in the lake had permeated her bones and now the chill from the earthen walls seeped into her from the outside, until she felt the same temperature and consistency, and possessing about as much brain matter, as the earth around her. This was really what it would have been like to be Antigone, she thought. This is what it would be like to be entombed.

Antigone had lost hope only moments before her husband-to-be came to find her. She had hanged herself with her linen veil moments before she would have been released. "Don't ever give up," she whispered to herself. *Don't ever give up.*

But her bones still ached with cold, and this damp chamber did nothing to warm her. Worse, a chilly draft circled her ankles and crept up the back of her legs.

But a draft? Where was that coming from? Overhead, the trap door was shut tight, so not from there. It felt as if it was coming from behind her.

Following the movement of air with her hands, she came to the tall wooden cupboard that stood against one wall of the room and out of which air seemed to be seeping. It was not so much a cupboard as a kind of wooden locker—a tall closet-like piece of furniture with no shelves inside. A wardrobe, that's what these things were called, Francie remembered.

She opened the door and tapped the back wall of the wardrobe. Was it her imagination, or did it sound hollow, as if there was nothing but air behind it? Was it possible this wardrobe served as a portal to, if not a magical world like Narnia, perhaps a way back to the land of the living?

Francie stepped inside the little closet and groped for a knob, a latch, a crack. Nothing. But when she tried sliding the back wall to the side, it budged, then slid open. The scent of pine and fallen leaves, lake and woods rushed in toward her: the smell of outside. But also the heavy smell of damp earth and clay. She wasn't outside yet.

Her first step forward did not lead into the familiar north-woods, but into more darkness, where what awaited her was seemingly nothing at all. Another step. And another. And yet another.

This must be a tunnel, she thought, her hands groping what felt like more plastic barrels, while under her feet, it seemed as if the ground was . . . sticky?

What was in these barrels? Why were they here? she wanted to know. But more urgently, she wanted to get the h-e-double-hockey-sticks out of there! And wasn't that a sliver of light ahead? The proverbial light at the end of the tunnel?

I've made it, I've escaped! she thought, just before there was an ominous thud, the light disappeared, and she heard the rustling of movement coming toward her.

"Theo?" she managed to croak out.

The only answer was a low, throaty laugh.

26

THE SITUATION GETS STICKY

A LIGHT FLICKED ON, the beam of which was immediately directed at Francie's face so she couldn't see who was coming toward her.

"Your life isn't worth a hill of beans," the figure behind the light said.

Who was that? Francie recognized the voice. She'd heard that same voice before. A man's voice.

Or—but no. It was not a man's voice. She'd heard the same voice in the lunch line. "Beans," that voice had said. A woman's voice. Evil Iris.

Something bright flashed in the beam of light, something that Francie recognized as the blade of a very large kitchen knife.

"I have a knife," Iris said.

"I see that," Francie replied.

"And I will use it unless you hand over that box."

"What do you want with it, anyway?" Francie said.

"Oh, I know all about it," she said. "I hear it all. When you're a cook or a server, you're invisible. Nobody pays any attention to you. People don't talk to you, unless they're asking for something. They talk to each other in front of you as if you aren't there. And they say things as if you aren't there. I keep my ears open and I hear things. Digby, he was like that—as if I wasn't there. I heard him say there was more back in these woods than mastodon bones. Something big. He mentioned a box. Then I heard you and your *bird* friend talking about it."

Bird friend? Oh, she meant Raven. They had talked in the lunch line, and Francie knew that there was truth in what Iris was saying. Francie mostly didn't think about the people behind the steam trays in the cafeteria. She didn't think about whether they were listening to conversations or not. She didn't think about them at all, come to think of it. She had never actually tried talking to Iris. She'd never thought Iris said more than one word at a time, and now she realized that Iris was not just a grouchy old lady—she was a *dangerous* old lady! And maybe not really that old either, and with forearms like Popeye's.

"So hand it over!" Iris said, moving closer.

"Tell me what happened to Theo first," Francie said, backing away.

"Seems to me that I'm the one with the knife," Iris said. "And I don't feel like telling you anything."

Francie couldn't swallow for a moment.

"Cat got your tongue?" Iris laughed that low, throaty laugh again, easily mistaken for a man's.

Was it possible that if you didn't see her when she spoke, you could think you'd heard a man? Things were not as they seemed, just as Mr. Redburn had said. Maybe Iris and the mystery man in the tent were the same person!

Francie knew she should run, but curiosity, and possibly fear and also probably stupidity, kept her rooted to the spot. "Look," she said, "tell me what's so special about the box, and I'll give it to you."

"You are one nosy kid," Iris said. "But not for much longer. It's really impossible to let you live now that you've been snooping around down here."

What happened next went so fast, Francie wouldn't have been able to explain it. Iris drew back her hand and lunged, but just before the knife would have made contact, Francie must have ducked, because the blade plunged instead into one of the barrels.

Again, Francie knew she should just get out of there, but now she noticed that sweet-smelling liquid was oozing from around the split in the barrel. The smell called up intense memories of breakfast, of pancakes, and of the moment in Muskie Bait when she'd bashed her assailant over the head with a can of . . . "Maple syrup?" Francie said. "Is *that* what's in these barrels? You would kill me because of some containers of maple syrup?"

"You wouldn't be the first." Iris grunted, tugging at the knife handle, the barrel unwilling to release its grasp of the blade.

"What? You mean . . . it was you? You killed Digby! Just because of some lousy maple syrup?"

Iris regained the knife and advanced as Francie retreated. "First of all," Iris said, "it isn't lousy. This is Grade A syrup—the very best Quebec has to offer."

"Why are you hiding it? It's not, like, illegal or anything," Francie said. "Or wait. Smuggling . . . Canada . . . it *is* illegal isn't it?"

"We needed to make some of the product 'disappear,' in a manner of speaking."

"Did you build this tunnel for that purpose?" Francie tried to imagine the undertaking.

"No, no." Iris chuckled again, which made Francie's flesh

creep. Just keep her talking, Francie thought. As long as she's talking, she's not killing me.

"This was a gold mine originally, from way back," Iris explained. "Then the bootleggers discovered it and used it to store their whiskey, and, well, here it was. I improved it and made use of it."

"And . . . ," Francie said, continuing her retreat, "you had to kill Digby because he was about to reveal all this to the sheriff?"

"The syrup was my brainchild. Digby didn't approve—didn't like it when he found out what I had stashed down here. 'Silly,' he called it—Silly!" Iris snorted derisively. "He thought his smuggling operation was serious, and mine was just silly."

"He had a smuggling operation, too?"

"Lordy, you are thick," Iris said.

"I have to say," Francie said, "I am disappointed. Somehow I thought it would be, I don't know, something bigger. I mean, maple syrup? How lame is that?"

This statement had a rage-inducing effect on Iris. "You need to learn some respect!" Iris growled, drawing back her arm once again.

Francie knew she should run; knew that Iris intended to kill her; knew that the likelihood of successfully dodging an attack again was slim; and yet it seemed her feet did not want to move. Her boots, she realized, were stuck to the ground.

The syrup! It had been leaking out of the torn barrel and mixing with the clay, and the floor of the tunnel had become a goopy morass. As the knife blade plunged toward her, Francie quite literally leapt out of her boots—thank goodness they were so big—and sprang, stocking-footed, away, down the tunnel the way she had come.

She was not alone; she could hear Iris sludging along after her. The light from Iris's headlamp illuminated the tunnel ahead, helping Francie in her flight, while also of course making her visible to her pursuer.

Francie reached the cupboard, still open, and leapt through it, back into the underground chamber. She found the ladder and began to climb, the box still clutched under her arm, aware of the flashlight beam playing below her.

Sticky fingers wrapped around her ankle and gave a jerk, making Francie almost tumble off the ladder. She let out a yelp, and the trapdoor overhead swung open; a hand gripped Francie's wrist and pulled. She felt her sock being pulled off her foot while from above strong arms lifted her up and out and set her on the wood floor—solid ground.

There followed a lot of hasty explanations mixed in with rope untangling and incoherent arguing.

"Shut the trap!" (That was Francie.) "She's right after me. Hurry up!"

"Help me get these ropes untied!" (That was Theo.)

"Shut the trap!" (Francie again.)

The trap was slammed shut, a table shoved on top of it, the ropes untangled, and Theo pulled Francie out the door. "We've got to get back to the cabin and call the sheriff!" he said.

"No!" Francie tugged on his arm. "We have to find the other end of the tunnel first, or she'll go out that way!"

"Sheriff!" Theo said.

"Tunnel!" Francie shouted, then said more slowly, "Ohhh . . . Roy . . ."

"Who's Roy?" Theo said.

"Jay's dog. I know where the tunnel comes out."

"What are you talking about?"

"Follow me!" she yelled, taking off down the path that led to the dig site.

While the still-stocking-footed Francie stumbled over roots

and rocks, Theo tried to explain that he'd been knocked out and tied up when she'd been underground.

"Theo," Francie said, her steps slowing, "am I hallucinating or whatever is the olfactory equivalent of hallucinating? I smell . . . turkey."

"And gravy," Theo added.

"And . . . pumpkin pie," Francie said. "Okay, that's it. Clearly we've both jumped the track."

Bounding down the path toward them came Roy, and then Raven and Jay, each holding a basket, as if about to embark on a lovely picnic.

"What are you guys doing here?" Francie asked. "And how did you get here?"

"Didn't you hear the helicopter?" Jay asked, and pointed to two official-looking men coming around the corner of the cabin wearing blue jackets printed with the letters *FBI*. "Those guys have access to everything," he said. Then, much to Francie's surprise, Mr. Redburn rounded the corner.

Francie looked on incredulously as Redburn and Theo greeted each other like old friends.

"Mr. Redburn?" Francie said.

"He works for the FBI, it turns out!" Jay said.

"And what a great cover!" Raven added. "High school drama coach! Who would suspect!"

Next the sheriff and two deputies appeared with Sandy.

"Can anybody explain to me what's going on?" Francie asked and then couldn't help but add, "And am I smelling turkey?" It smelled so delicious she thought she might faint.

"And gravy?" Theo added.

"Yeah, that's what's in here," Jay said, holding up his picnic basket.

27

THANKSGIVING DINNER

LATER, after a very sticky Iris was taken away by the FBI, and Francie's feet had thawed out by the fire, Theo, Francie, Raven, Jay, Sandy, Mr. Redburn, and his fiancée, Sheriff Warner, plus the sheriff's deputies, all sat down to a belated but much appreciated Thanksgiving dinner.

"We usually put some maple syrup on the sweet potatoes," Jay apologized, "but we didn't have any."

"Oh," Francie said, "I know where you can get syrup. All you would ever want."

"So," the sheriff turned to Francie, "explain to me how you knew Iris was the killer."

"It wasn't until today when I heard her say, 'Beans,' that I knew she had been at the dig site the night of Digby's murder."

"Beans," the sheriff repeated, squinting at Francie.

"Beans!" Raven shouted from the kitchen. "Iris says that in the lunch line." Raven came out carrying a casserole dish. "As in, 'Do you want some beans?'" She handed Francie the dish and said, "Um, do you want some beans?"

Francie helped herself to the green bean casserole and went on. "And today when I heard that same voice say, 'Your life isn't worth a hill of beans,' I remembered I'd heard something similar in Digby's tent the day of his murder."

"And you didn't think to tell me about this?" the sheriff asked Francie.

Francie was silent. She knew she had been wrong to withhold information. The case might even have been solved faster had she been more forthcoming. She resolved to be honest from now on, and a kind of relief swept over her.

"In the tent, the day of the murder, I heard someone arguing with Digby," she said. "Same exact voice, but I thought it was a man's, so I didn't put two and two together."

"But absolutely no one saw Iris here the day of the murder."

"Right," Francie said. "And she's not a woman you don't notice. But she had an unusual way to get to the site without being seen."

"How is that?"

"That tunnel. It leads from an old shack behind the Johnsons' cabin to the dig site."

"Maybe an old gold mine," Jay said. "And then used during Prohibition to hide liquor."

"No kidding?" the sheriff said. She glanced out the window. "We'll have to go take a look. So let me get this straight. Digby discovered the tunnel and the smuggled goods, then called me, intending to reveal all this, but Iris killed him before he could do that. She came and went through the tunnel, and that is why nobody saw her."

"Right. But . . . ," Francie said. "I still don't get it. All that because of some maple syrup?"

"Might have been a lot of syrup," the sheriff said. "Six million pounds have gone missing from the Global Strategic Maple Syrup Reserve."

"The what?" Raven asked.

"Yep. You heard me. Quebec produces something like three-quarters of the world's maple syrup. In good years, they stockpile some in what is called the Global Strategic Maple Syrup Reserve. There was a really good year recently, so there was a lot of syrup stored in a warehouse in Canada. Someone figured out how to pull off a really good heist and made off with six million pounds of it."

"But there can't be that much down there in the tunnels!"

"No," the sheriff said. "Iris was only a small wheel in a bigger machine. The masterminds were probably trying to squirrel away smaller amounts until they could get it to market. I think they were trying to get some of it out of circulation and did some distributing."

"Why would anyone go to the trouble of hiding it way out here in the boonies, though?" Francie asked.

"Are you kidding?" Sandy said. "This side of the lake is a great place to hide something, summer or winter. In the winter, nobody's here to ask questions, so things can be moved over the lake by snowmobile, and smugglers just look like ice fishermen. Great place to stash the syrup this past summer, too. Nice and cool underground, and what with all the workers from the dig coming and going, there was so much boat traffic, who would notice one more boat? Or one more barrel being loaded onto and off a boat—especially by the cook, right?"

"Is it possible Iris may have been involved in other smuggling, too?" Francie asked. "Because, I mean, maple syrup! Come on!"

"Yes," the sheriff conceded, "that is of course a possibility, and we'll be looking into it. Digby was suspected of a much bigger kind of smuggling operation."

"Which may still be going on," Redburn added, "except Digby isn't part of it anymore."

"Anybody for pie?" Jay asked, emerging from the kitchen with a steaming pumpkin pie.

The deputies looked longingly at it, but the sheriff shook her head. "We need to get going," she said, picking up her hat from the table near the door.

Francie said, "You know . . . do you suppose it'd be possible, as you're loading bones onto the barge, to be unloading other bones?"

"What do you mean?"

"How many pounds of mastodon bones do you think were loaded onto the barge to be shipped to the university?" Francie asked anybody who might know.

"Couple thousand pounds, I should guess," Redburn said.

"And how many pounds would a very large dinosaur skeleton be?"

"The missing bones the FBI are looking for right now amount to three thousand pounds," Redburn said.

Theo added that the skeleton, when assembled, "would be about eight feet tall and twenty-four feet long."

"Just wondering . . . ," Francie mused.

"If that missing dinosaur skeleton . . . ," Redburn continued.

"Might be found in some crates with a lot of mastodon bones . . . ," Theo said excitedly.

"At the university?" Raven suggested.

"Or even around here somewhere, I wonder," the sheriff said. "If there are more tunnels—"

"It's also possible," Theo said, bringing everybody back to earth, "that only Digby knows where that skeleton is."

"And he's dead," Jay stated the obvious.

"Well," the sheriff said at last, putting on her hat. "We'd better be getting back."

"How did you get here, anyway?" Francie asked.

"The lake is open around the point," Sandy explained. He stood, slipped into his jacket, and held the door for the sheriff, deputies, and Redburn.

But the sheriff turned back and said thoughtfully, "What was Iris doing out here, anyway? I mean, why now?"

Francie and Theo exchanged a glance, then simultaneously said, "No idea."

The sheriff gave them a little squint, then turned and went out.

After they were gone, Francie turned to Raven and Jay and asked, "How did you guys know to come?"

"Raven and I decided to combine our leftovers and bring them out to you somehow or other," Jay answered. "We were going to cross that ice when we got to it, so to speak. But as we were putting the food together, we also got to putting two and two together."

"It was the food, see?" Raven chimed in. "I started thinking about that cook tent and the missing knife. It was there, then it wasn't, yet there wasn't any mention of anyone finding it at the dig site. Who would go into the cook tent and take a big knife, especially from Evil Iris? Would you? No. Nobody would! So Iris must have taken it herself, which meant she must have been there—at the dig site—somehow or other. Then I remembered when we were in the lunch line that we had discussed both the murder and the . . . well," she said, stifling the word *box*, and saying again, "*the murder*, and I got worried, and I just thought, Geez, we better go out there and make sure everything's okay."

"But how did you convince the sheriff and—for the love of Mike!—the FBI to come out here?"

"Oh, we didn't convince them," Raven said. "That was just a lucky break for us. They got a tip that the smuggled syrup was over here and were planning to investigate. They didn't know Iris had anything to do with it. It was a lucky break for them that she was here and so messily incriminated herself."

"You know what, Raven?" Francie said. "You are a much better detective than I am."

"What?" Raven said. "No! You solved the murder."

"I just stumbled onto it," Francie protested. "You actually figured it out."

"Well, let's just say we're a good team," Raven said.

From across the room, Jay looked a little forlorn until Francie added, "You, too, Jay—we couldn't have done it without you."

Jay smiled, his rosy cheeks glowing.

"But if you want to be taken seriously," Raven said, "you're going to have to get that glob of mashed potatoes out of your hair."

The warm food, warm cabin, the hum of the conversation, and the sound of dishes being washed and put away—these things plus the relief that comes after a protracted trauma all conspired to make Francie very drowsy.

She leaned her head on Theo's shoulder and murmured, "What about that tooth, Theo?"

"Tooth?" he said.

"You know what I'm talking about," Francie said.

"That was Digby that chased us the night of Muskie Bait."

"I know," Francie said.

"How?"

"It was the trench coat that gave it away, but never mind that. Explain why you had that tooth."

"That dino tooth belonged to the skeleton that Digby stole. He was anxious to get it back, and he had information about Mom. That tooth was going to be my bargaining chip, so to speak. Redburn will make sure the tooth gets back with the rest of the skeleton—if and when the skeleton is found, that is."

Francie let her eyes close. There was something else she wanted to talk to Theo about, but she was warm and well fed, the voices in the kitchen and the soft clatter of dishes being washed were like a lullaby, and she felt her mind drifting.

Of course she was not aware that she had fallen asleep. Nor was she aware of Theo carrying her off to her aunts' bed and tucking her in under the warm comforter, while the others rolled out sleeping bags on the cabin floor.

Perhaps it was the soft tapping at the window that woke her, much later, after everyone was asleep. She climbed out of bed and stepped over the sleeping bodies of Raven and Jay, curled up in their respective sleeping bags on the floor. In the light of the glowing embers of the fire, she found her way to the window and stood looking out at the snow that had begun to fall, silently accumulating on every branch and twig, covering the ice-covered bay like a woolen blanket, and turning the whole world white. A young birch, bent from the weight of the snow, arched like a dinosaur's long neck, its crown the beast's head, dripping icicle teeth. Among branches swollen with snow, she saw a forest transformed into the bleached bones of dinosaurs: branches became rib bones, twigs were claws and talons. Not fearful but beautiful. And somehow peaceful.

She turned to see Theo on the couch, the silver box in his hands. She sat down next to him and he gave it to her. For the first time she was able to examine the intricate engravings on its sides.

"Trees!" she exclaimed, tracing the thickly growing trunks and delicately entwined branches that wove around all four sides and over the top of the silver box. "I've always thought, irrationally, I know," Francie said, "that my heart was inside this box. But now that you're here, and I've made some nice friends, and I feel at home . . . I think my heart is back where it belongs."

Theo took her hand and said, "I'm glad."

"But what is this thing, really?" she asked. "And why is it so important?"

"This," he said, "is a box full of secrets. We'll try to figure it all out—tomorrow. For now, we should probably get some sleep. Soon enough, danger will be coming our way."

AUTHOR'S NOTE

Warning: it would be better if you read this after reading the story.

The Clue in the Trees is a work of fiction, but many of the current or historical episodes, events, and issues in the story are based on real things or true stories. Mammoths, bootlegging, gold rushes, mining, and pipelines are all things that Minnesota has experienced or is facing right now.

MAMMOTHS, UNKTEHI, DRAGON BONES

During the Mesozoic era, a period of time 252 million to 66 million years ago, mastodons and woolly mammoths roamed nearly everywhere on earth—including Minnesota.

Ever since, people have been finding their bones and trying to make sense of them. Raven tells Francie that in early times, the Dakota (Sioux) of Minnesota attributed these bones to a water monster called Unktehi, a creature that resembled a giant buffalo. The bones were thought to have a powerful supernatural potency. Medicine men chewed on them as part of their initiation and kept pieces of the bones in their medicine bags. Now paleontologists believe that the bones they found were those of mastodons.

Jay learns in his research that in China "dragon bones" (which are actually mammoth, mastodon, and dinosaur bones) are still consumed for a variety of ailments ranging from hypertension and stroke to "dream-disturbed sleep."

Jay also mentions that many endangered animals are illegally killed for their supposed medicinal value: rhinoceroses are slaughtered for their horns and tigers for their bones. Ninety-seven percent of the world's tiger population has been exterminated, and rhinos are fast disappearing. Sun bears and Asiatic black bears are killed for their paws and bile. Seahorse populations are rapidly declining because they are used in traditional medicines. And pangolins, small ant-eating, scale-covered mammals, are at the top of the most endangered mammal groups in the world.

GOLD AND OTHER MINING IN MINNESOTA

Northern Minnesota was the scene of two minor gold rushes in 1865–66 and 1893. The small amount of gold found was more expensive to extract than it was worth, and the two rushes were short-lived. The Little American Mine on Little American Island in Rainy Lake was the only productive gold mine in Minnesota. Abandoned mine shafts are still apparent on the island. The rush helped develop the settlement of International Falls as well as other communities in northern Minnesota. The Minnesota Department of Natural Resources has recently reported "significant gold findings" along the historic Vermilion Iron Range. Dozens of test mine shafts have been drilled and leases have been offered to prospectors and companies that might be interested in extracting it.

Iron was discovered on the Iron Range in 1866 and proved a better bet and far more lucrative than gold. Although iron mining in Minnesota has slowed since its heyday, it still continues today, although with a lower grade of ore being extracted.

Now copper-nickel mining is being proposed in northern Minnesota. Those who support it hope it will bring back jobs that were lost as iron mining waned. Those who oppose it point out that copper-nickel mining is too environmentally dangerous, much more so than iron mining, especially in northern Minnesota where these mines will be situated near so many waterways. The waste from this kind of mining creates sulfuric acid that can (as it often has elsewhere) contaminate lakes, streams, and wetlands and create long-term damage to ecosystems.

BOOTLEGGING

Northern Minnesota, especially near the Canadian border, was the scene of liquor smuggling, or "bootlegging," when alcohol was illegal in the United States during Prohibition (1920–33). You can read more about bootlegging on Rainy Lake in northern Minnesota in Mary Casanova's suspenseful novel *Ice-Out*.

GLOBAL STRATEGIC MAPLE SYRUP RESERVE AND HEIST

Nearly 80 percent of the world's maple syrup supply comes from the province of Quebec in Canada. In 2012, six million pounds of maple syrup worth eighteen million dollars went missing from Quebec's Global Strategic Maple Syrup Reserve. (Yes, that is a real thing.) Canada's excess maple syrup was being stored in a warehouse in Quebec. In an inside job, the thieves rented part of the warehouse as a way to get to the syrup and managed to make off with sixteen thousand barrels of syrup by emptying barrels into other barrels and leaving the empties—or sometimes refilling the emptied containers with water. Most of the syrup went to New Brunswick and was eventually recovered, but quite a bit was smuggled into the United States, where it may have ended up on your pancakes.

OIL PIPELINES

Minnesota, like many places in the United States, struggles with how to transport oil. Crude oil is transported either by rail or by pipeline from its source (in the case of this story, the Bakken Fields in North Dakota, where oil is extracted by fracking). Some people believe that pipelines are a safer way to transport oil than by rail, but others think the environmental risk of pipelines are too great, especially in Minnesota where pipelines travel through so many environmentally sensitive areas. The Sandpiper Pipeline (currently on hold) would have passed through twenty-eight rivers, including the headwaters of the Mississippi; many of these areas are remote and unpopulated, so a leak could go undetected for a long time. Spilled oil can quickly pollute waterways, contaminate drinking water, kill fish, and damage entire ecosystems.

Because of these issues, protests have occurred in many places where oil pipelines have been proposed. In addition to protests against the proposed Sandpiper Pipeline, a very large protest took place near Standing Rock Reservation in North Dakota, where the Dakota Access Pipeline was supposed to pass under Lake Oahe (part of the Missouri River), the main source of drinking water for nearby populations. Though the protests delayed it, construction is moving ahead at the time of this writing.

In the story, Raven stood up for what she believed in and educated others (including Francie), who consequently became interested and got involved. You can make a difference, too. Find your issue! Get involved!

ACKNOWLEDGMENTS

Many thanks to the knowledgeable people who read this book as I was writing and who offered sage advice or helpful life experience, including Wendy Savage, Kathy Bogen, Carolyn Olson, Mary Preus, Catherine Preus, Ann Treacy, and Corrine Roy. I'm also grateful to Anders Hanson for the clue-filled cover art and to all the fine folks at the University of Minnesota Press, especially Erik Anderson.

Margi Preus is the award-winning author of several books for young readers, including *Enchantment Lake* (Minnesota, 2015), *West of the Moon, Shadow on the Mountain, The Bamboo Sword,* and the Newbery Honor book *Heart of a Samurai.* The Enchantment Lake mysteries were written on the screen porch of her cabin, which overlooks a lake remarkably like the one in the stories.